MW00849640

FATAL FARMING

A BETH AND EVIE MYSTERY: BOOK 3

FATAL FARMING

A BETH AND EVIE MYSTERY: BOOK 3

BONNIE OLDRE

gatekeeper press
Tampa, Florida

This book is a work of fiction. The names, characters, and events in this book are the products of the author's imagination or are used fictitiously. Any similarity to real persons living or dead is coincidental and not intended by the author.

The content associated with this book is the sole work and responsibility of the author. Gatekeeper Press had no involvement in the generation of this content.

Fatal Farming

Published by Gatekeeper Press
7853 Gunn Hwy., Suite 209
Tampa, FL 33626
www.GatekeeperPress.com

Copyright © 2024 by Bonnie Oldre
All rights reserved. Neither this book nor any parts within it may be sold or reproduced in any form or by any electronic or mechanical means, including information storage and retrieval systems, without permission in writing from the author. The only exception is by a reviewer, who may quote short excerpts in a review.

Library of Congress Control Number: 2024942807

ISBN (paperback): 9781662951404
eISBN: 9781662951411

Contents

Chapter 1

June 28, 1969

Beth stood outside of the Majestic Theater in Davison City, Minnesota with her best friend Evie. The temperature was in the nineties, and the humidity was nearly as high. They held bottles of Orange Crush—it was that or Fresca, which they would only drink if it was the only thing available.

The Majestic, an old movie theater, had been closed for several years. Logan Rusk, the new owner, had plans to reopen it as a live theater. It might have been majestic once, but even when Beth went there to see movies as a kid, it was getting run-down. It was located on the edge of the commercial area, a block from the church in one direction and a block from the library in the other direction. Now, with the library closed on Saturdays in the summer, there wasn't much traffic.

Beth rolled the cool bottle over her forehead. "Can you believe how hot it is in the middle of June? What a miserable day for painting," she said. "I'd much rather be lying on a beach blanket next to a lake."

"Me too. Sorry I roped you into this. When Logan asked me to volunteer, I thought it would be more fun if you joined me. I had no idea it would be this hot and sticky." Evie sighed and took a swig from her bottle. "But I guess they need to paint the lobby before they can install the new carpeting. Are you sorry you came?"

"Kind of." Beth laughed. "Just kidding! It's more fun than doing my laundry, which is what I planned to do this Saturday afternoon, not go to the beach. Hey, remember when we used to come here for Saturday matinees in the summer?"

"Sure. It was the only cool place in town. We'd sit through anything, just to stay cool. They had air-conditioning then. I suppose it still does, but it must not be working."

Just then, Logan came out to join them, also carrying a bottle of pop that was dripping with condensation.

"Wow, it's steamy in there! You ladies have the right idea. I have a guy coming out this week to get the air-conditioning working, if it's not beyond repair. Say, thanks again for helping me out. I don't know what I'd do without you. There's a ton of work that needs to be done before we open." He smiled at them.

Beth thought that he was very handsome, in a slightly disheveled way. He had a sheepish grin, big brown eyes behind horn-rimmed glasses, and tousled, dark, curly hair. He wore a Hawaiian shirt over jeans, and sandals. He looked much as he had when he was in high school. Except, his face was leaner;

there were a few creases around his eyes and a few gray hairs around the temples. She wondered about the slightly haunted look he had when he wasn't smiling. She'd heard about the traffic accident that had killed his wife a few years ago. She supposed that was the cause.

"So, the library is closed on Saturdays in the summer?" he said to Beth.

"Yup. I get weekends off. I do a couple afternoon into evening shifts and drive our new bookmobile one day a week."

"Well, I'd better get back to work," Logan said. "No rest for the wicked. We're starting auditions today. Can you stick around for pizza later?"

They said that would be great, and he disappeared back into the theater.

After he left, Evie said, "I thought they were going to give you more hours at the library because of the money they got from the sale of the antique Shakespeare books we found."

"I wish. But the library board said one-time money wouldn't work for ongoing expenses, like salaries. They spent it all on the bookmobile I drive instead. Well, most of it. Some of it was earmarked for a small special collection that I manage, which is also fun."

"Makes sense, I guess. And, I'm glad you have more time off to do fun stuff, like paint a theater." Evie laughed. "How do you like driving the bookmobile?"

"It's great."

"Where do you go?"

"To small towns that don't have their own libraries. I have a regular route. The librarian, Miss Tanner, arranged everything. I park in a church or school parking lots. It's fun to see the kids checking out armloads of library books."

"Like we did when we were kids," Evie said.

"Exactly. I just thought of something! Once the theater is up and running, I can put posters in the bookmobile advertising the season and draw people from the surrounding area." Beth stepped back and looked up at the theater. "Did you know that this was originally an opera house before it was converted into a movie theater?"

"No. So it came full circle; an opera house, a movie theater, and now it's going to be a live theater again."

"Yeah. It'll be exciting to have live theater here in town."

"Do you think Logan can make it work? After all, it went out of business as a movie theater, and I'm guessing movies are more popular than plays," Evie said.

"True, but there are only so many movies being made. I guess this town couldn't sustain two movie theaters. I think it'll succeed. After all, people want to get out of the house and go someplace. And this will be another option," Beth said.

"I hope you're right. Rumor has it that Logan put everything he has into the project. He even took out a second mortgage on his house to buy the place," Evie said.

"No kidding? Where'd you hear that?"

"Not sure. Somebody heard Logan talking to the bank on the phone."

"Logan mortgaged his home! He must be really determined. Well, he's young and single now."

Evie paused. "Single now . . . yeah, I think that's the key. He and Angela were big movie buffs when they were dating, always sitting in the back, holding hands every Saturday night."

"Really? I guess I didn't pay that much attention. But you dated, right?"

"Yeah. He was two years ahead of us in school. I met him when we were in theater together. I was a sophomore and he was a senior."

"That's right. I remember now. An older man—how could you resist?"

"I couldn't." Evie laughed. "We dated a few times, but it didn't last. I guess he really wasn't my type. Then I met Jim."

A black Cadillac caught their attention as it braked sharply, pulled up to the curb, and parked. Beth and Evie watched a thirty-something stocky guy, sporting a crewcut and a short-sleeved shirt, hop out and race towards the theater, swinging his arms, fist clenched.

"Who's that?" Beth asked.

"Him? That's our would-be local celebrity, Vern Cedar."

"Who?" The name didn't ring any bells for Beth.

"He does a weekly radio show on KROW, calls himself Red Cedar on the air."

"Oh yeah, him—the obnoxious twit who gets people to call in on the radio and then insults them," Beth said.

Evie laughed at the description. "One and the same."

Vern skidded to a halt in front of them. He leered at the tall, willowy Evie.

Beth reflected that Evie looked cute in her paint-splattered t-shirt and cutoff jeans, with her long blonde hair in a braid hanging down her back. While she, though similarly dressed, undoubtedly did not. She was shorter and plumper than Evie, with unruly light-brown wavy hair that was currently escaping from her headband and sticking to her sweaty neck.

Vern focused on Evie and didn't seem to notice Beth. "Hi, doll. Do I know you?" he asked Evie.

"I don't know. Do you?" Evie said.

"You're one of the Hanson kids. Evie Hanson, right?"

"Yup, that's me." Evie turned toward Beth. "Beth, this charming fellow is Vernon Cedar. Vernon, this is my friend, Beth Williams. Vern graduated from high school a few years ahead of us. At least I think he did." Turning back to Vern, she said, "Remind me. You graduated from high school, right?"

Vern laughed, as though this was hilarious. "Yup. By the skin of my teeth. Is the theater impresario in?" He gestured toward the theater.

"Who?" Evie asked.

"The impresario, the new owner of this magnificent establishment, Logan Rusk."

"I don't know." Evie shrugged.

He turned to Beth, seeming to notice her for the first time. "Have you seen him?"

"I think he's in there," Beth said. "Is he expecting you?"

Vern narrowed his eyes and glared at her. "Is that any of your business?"

Beth, slightly shocked, stared at him for a moment before she answered. "You're kind of rude, aren't you? I suppose that's an advantage for a—what is it that you are—an insult comedian or something?"

"I'm a farmer with a little radio talk show on the side. That is, it's little right now but growing in popularity by leaps and bounds. Sure to be the next big thing. Have you listened to it?" he said.

"I caught a bit of the show, *once*," Beth said.

"Just once, huh? Not your cup of tea?"

"Nope. I thought it was . . ." Beth searched for a description. "Embarrassing."

Vern flushed. "You should listen again. Maybe you'll change your mind. In fact, I'm thinking of doing a show on this new endeavor." He waved his hand toward the theater. "You should join me. I'd love to chat with you on the air."

"I don't think so," Beth said. "Why would I?"

Vern tried to laugh it off. "It would be good publicity. And I have my fans. Different strokes, I guess."

"Yeah, well, I'm just a volunteer. I'm not the person to talk to about publicity," Beth said.

"How about you, doll?" he said, turning to Evie.

"The name is Evie. And, my answer is the same as Beth's. We're just here to help a friend."

"I can be your friend, too, if you come on my show," he said.

"A tempting offer, but no thanks," Evie said.

With a stiff smile, he said, "Well, the offer stands if you change your mind. Meanwhile, I can't hang around shooting the breeze all day. Ladies." He nodded to them, turned, and strode into the theater.

Once he was out of earshot, Evie and Beth looked at each other, rolled their eyes, and laughed.

Sobering up, Beth said, "What a jerk! I would have told him that Logan and Nigel are conducting auditions if he'd been halfway civil."

"Oh, that's right. I forgot." Evie took a swig of pop and then frowned. "I just hope he doesn't talk about us on his show."

"Would he?" Beth asked.

"Of course. He lives for conversations he can repeat on the air. Only, in his version the other people come off as village idiots, and he's the smart one."

"And people listen to that?"

"They sure do. He models himself after Joe Pyne, who's extremely popular. Heard of him?"

"I think so. He does a TV show, right? I haven't seen it, but I read a piece about him in a news magazine. They said he got his start on the radio, where he kind of invented a whole new genre. He was taking song requests and started arguing with the folks who called in, and it caught on. They said he goes for the shock value."

"True. My brothers are big fans. So, I've caught some of his show."

"So, Vern is trying to hop on that bandwagon. But a weekly radio show can't be very lucrative. I guess that's why he's also a farmer."

"He was a farmer first. As I recall, he inherited his place."

"Farmer and insult disc jockey. That's quite the combo. I wonder if he insults his livestock."

Beth and Evie laughed at the idea.

"I don't know about his animals, but I hear he's pretty hard on his neighbors. A bunch of hippies moved in down the road from him, and he's always going on about them," Evie said.

"I wonder why he's here."

"Probably looking for trouble," Evie said.

After they finished their drinks, they went inside and resumed painting. The door of the Majestic was propped open, and a large floor fan sat just inside of the door. It rattled away, set on high in a futile attempt to blow fresh air into the lobby. The noise of the fan and the high-pitched chatter and laughter of a group of teen volunteers working on the other side of the lobby rendered normal conversational levels impossible. So, Beth didn't immediately realize that Vern and Logan were standing behind them until they started shouting over the noise.

Beth turned in their direction, her paintbrush held midair, forgotten, as it dripped green paint on the drop cloth under her feet.

"Come on my program as my guest, and I'll give you a chance to talk it up," Vern said. "Call it free publicity."

"I would welcome publicity, but I know you, Vern. You're looking for a chance to ridicule me and the theater, not to give us publicity."

Vern smiled and said something in low tones that Beth didn't catch.

"Very funny!" Logan said. "That's not true, and you know it. If you spoil our opening, I'll . . . I'll . . . I don't know what I'll do."

Vern laughed and then imitated him. "'I'll . . . I'll . . .' You're sputtering, Logan. I'm not spoiling anything."

Their voices sank, and Beth didn't hear what was said until Vern laughed a nasty, barking laugh and then shouted, "What's the matter? Scared? Don't you think you can handle whatever I throw at you, Logan? If you want to get people talking about your little theater, being a guest on my show is your best bet. Think it over."

Logan turned and walked away from him. Vern stood looking after him for a moment, a triumphant sneer on his face. He turned and began to stride toward the exit.

He stopped and his face fell when an attractive brunette in her mid-thirties, with her hair tied back in a ponytail, came through the door. They stopped and stared at each other for a moment. He grabbed her by the arm and pulled her out of the theater. Beth turned to Evie, who had also been watching and listening.

"What was that all about?" she shouted.

Evie shrugged.

A few moments later, the woman came back in. She paused and looked at the cardboard sign saying "Auditions This Way" with an arrow pointing into the body of the theater and walked in that direction, disappearing through the swinging double doors.

Vern rushed back into the theater, following her. A few minutes later he returned, red-faced and scowling, with

Logan following him. They disappeared into Logan's office. A few moments later, they came out of the office. Vern strode through the theater lobby and left, and Logan went back into the theater.

Evie leaned towards Beth and said, "That was Vern's wife, Ruth. I wonder what she was doing here."

"Auditioning, I suppose. And I guess Vern's not too thrilled about it."

Relaxing backstage, Beth took a bite of pizza. It was a bit bland and not very hot. But at least it was pizza. "When did they open a pizza restaurant in town?" she asked Evie.

"Last year," Evie said. "Do you like it?"

"Love it. I'm famished after an afternoon of spilling paint on myself."

Logan walked past the table of giggling high-school-age volunteers, carrying a sagging paper plate of pizza in one hand and a can of beer in the other, and sat across the battered folding table from Beth and Evie. A taller, balding man, wearing a floral shirt with the top two buttons open and the sleeves rolled up, followed Logan. He deposited his food and beer on the table and sat next to him.

"Evie, I think you've met our director, Nigel?" Logan said.

Evie nodded and raised a hand in greeting. Her mouth was full of pizza.

"And this is Evie's friend, Beth Williams. They volunteered to help us with some painting today," Logan said.

"Pleased to meet you," Beth said.

"Nigel has experience in the theater," Logan said. "We met through mutual friends, and I twisted his arm to come up here and give me a hand with this new enterprise. He represents the entirety of our paid staff at the moment." Logan laughed.

"Wonderful," Beth said. "Did you drive up for the auditions?"

Nigel smiled back at Beth. "Actually, I drove up last night, and I'll be heading back home tonight. I'll be back next weekend."

"Nigel lives in the Twin Cities," Logan said. "Beth, you used to live in the Twin Cities too, right?"

"Yup, I went there for college and stayed for a while," Beth said. "Now I'm back in my hometown."

"How do you like being back home?" Nigel asked.

"Good, so far. I enjoy spending time with my family and reconnecting with old friends. And, I'm also working on a master's in Library Science and have a part-time job in the library."

Beth and Nigel chatted for a while about the Twin Cities' neighborhoods and theaters.

"I'll be going back and forth for the next couple of months. I've got things to wind up," Nigel said. "I hope to move here before we start rehearsals in the fall."

Logan looked at Beth and Evie, paused, and then said, "I guess you overheard part of that conversation I had earlier with Vern?"

They nodded.

"What's this about?" Nigel asked.

Logan gave him a brief recap.

"So, what do you all think? Should I take him up on the offer of being a guest on his radio show? Is it worth the risk?"

Nigel looked at them, eyebrows raised. "I guess I don't have the big picture. Why is it a risk?"

"Vern is kind of a jerk. He tried to blackmail me into coming on the show by threatening to reveal some of my youthful indiscretions if I didn't," Logan said. Logan explained Vern's radio show. "He was a bully in high school, and now he's making it into a career."

"Is he the jerk who interrupted our audition?" Nigel asked.

"Yup, that's him," Logan said.

"What's the deal with that? Was that his wife or his girlfriend?" Nigel asked.

"His wife. And I gather he doesn't want her to audition. But she's really pretty good. Don't you agree?" Logan said.

"She was good. We'll have to see who else auditions for the part. But I don't think we can let what Mr. Cedar thinks influence our decision." Nigel paused for a bite of pizza.

"They'll have to work it out between themselves. I suppose we can get her assurance that her husband won't cause us any more trouble before we cast her."

"That sounds good," Logan said. "Meanwhile, what do you all think? Should I go on his show or not? On one hand, it *is* free publicity. On the other, it will just reward him for making threats, and I'm sure he'll try to make an ass out of me for the amusement of his listening audience."

"But you can just laugh it off. Can't you?" Nigel said. "It seems like any publicity is better than none."

"What do you think?" Logan asked Beth and Evie.

"I guess we could always walk out if he gets too obnoxious," Evie said.

"We?" Logan asked. "Are you saying we should both go?"

"Not just you and me—the three of us—you, me, and Beth." Evie made an inclusive motion. "Vern asked Beth and me before he talked to you. We were taking a break outside the theater when Vern first got here. He stopped to talk and asked if we wanted to be on his show."

"What did you say?" Logan asked.

"We told him we're just volunteers and that he should talk to you." Evie turned toward Beth. "The three of us could go together. Right, Beth?"

"Maybe," Beth said.

"What's the worst that could happen?" Nigel asked. "Even if he's obnoxious, at least a few people will hear about a new theater that's opening soon. Right?"

"What do you think, Beth?" Evie asked.

Beth grimaced. "I'm not sure. I didn't get a good vibe off Vern. Logan is probably right that he'll try to make fools of us. But I also think that Nigel is right. Any publicity is better than none. I'd go if you two decide you want to do it."

After some more pizza and discussion, they agreed to do the interview. Logan said he'd call Vern and get back to them about the details.

Chapter 2

June 29-30, 1969

On Sunday afternoon, Beth and Evie sat on the couch in Beth's apartment and sipped iced tea while Chestnut, Beth's cat, slept between them. A breeze from the open window wafted over the top of the terrarium sitting on her bookcase, carrying with it the sound of a distant lawnmower and the scent of newly cut grass. It had rained overnight, washing out the heat and humidity. Beth glanced at the violets in the terrarium, wondering if they were getting too much sun.

Evie followed her glance. "They look happy there on top of your new bookcase."

"I hope they like it better there than in the kitchen. Maybe they'll even start to bloom."

"Is that the bookcase your dad made for you?" Evie got up and examined it. "He sure did a nice job."

"I know." Beth rattled the ice cubes in her glass to stir up the sugar that had settled on the bottom, took a sip, and sighed. "What have we signed up for?"

"You mean the Red Cedar radio show? Are you having second thoughts?" Evie said.

"Yeah. You know he'll try to embarrass us. That seems to be his shtick. How does that help Logan, the Majestic Theater, or anyone? I doubt there's a big overlap between Cedar's listeners and theatergoers."

"Probably not." Evie paused and frowned. "He claimed he's not out to get us, not that I trust anything he says. Either way, it's free PR. If he lets us talk about the upcoming theater season—great. If he tries to stir up controversy, and things get confrontational, then word will spread beyond his audience. Anyway, we don't have anything to hide. Do we?"

"Doesn't everybody?" Beth said. "I have no idea what he has up his sleeve. If nothing else, he'll probably point out that the movie theater went broke and that the new enterprise is doomed to fail too," Beth said.

"I don't know if he'll take that line. That doesn't sound too entertaining or controversial. Just in case, Miss Information, why don't you look up some statistics about the number of theaters in Minnesota or that have opened recently. We can bore him with numbers if he tries that tactic."

"Who are you calling misinformation?" Beth chuckled. "But that's a good idea. I'll see what I can find."

* * *

Beth got up early on Monday morning to get to the library and fill the bookmobile with books. Driving the bookmobile was still new and exciting. She wanted to be sure she got to her first stop on time.

A twenty-minute drive north took her to her first stop, Plato. It was a town of a few hundred people. The few businesses were laid out on one side of the highway, across from the grain elevators and railroad tracks. When she pulled into St. Mary's parking lot, she was pleased to see a few kids sitting on the curb, waiting for her, holding small stacks of books they'd checked out last week.

The next couple of hours flew by as she checked books in and out, talked to the kids, and an occasional mother, about books—which ones they liked best and why. Beth jotted down notes, compiling a list of the books they checked out, cross-referencing them by author and genre, and adding asterisks next the ones they mentioned as favorites in order to supply more of what they liked.

As it got close to noon, Beth began to reshelve books and stow everything away to close up for lunch and then move on to the next town on her route. Just then, a dusty and exhausted-looking young woman pushing a battered baby carriage turned into the parking lot and ran in her direction. Her long empire waist dress swirled around her legs as she ran, and her long blonde hair swung loosely around her face.

"Hello, hello," she called out as she trotted in Beth's direction. "Wait for us. Don't close yet!"

"That's okay. You don't have to run. I can wait," Beth called back. She watched as the young woman slowed and approached at a brisk walk. When they got closer, Beth noticed a blond baby boy, who looked to be about six months old, sleeping in the stroller. He was slumped sideways, and his cheeks were bright red.

The young mother started to lift the stroller into the van.

"Here, let me help," Beth said. She reached down and pulled up on the stroller's handle while the girl lifted it from the front.

Once it was inside, the young woman clambered up after it.

"Thanks," she panted. She looked around for somewhere to sit and then slumped down onto the low, built-in bench over the heater, located behind the driver's seat, and pulled the baby carriage close to her. "It was a longer walk than I thought it was."

Beth took a closer look at her. She was thin, around eighteen or nineteen years old, and looked hot and dusty.

"Do you want something to drink?" Beth asked.

"That would be great," she said.

Beth poured a cup of coffee from her thermos and handed it to her. "Sorry, this is all I have—not too refreshing, I'm afraid." She made a mental note to bring cold beverages for library patrons on future trips—maybe in a small cooler.

"Thanks. This is great," the girl said and then gulped some down.

"My name is Beth Williams," Beth said.

"Nice to meet you. My name is Sunshine and this is Silas." She brushed the baby's long, blond bangs off of his forehead. "Oh no, I think he might have a fever." She looked up at Beth with worried eyes.

Beth reached down and touched his forehead. "He *is* a little warm. Maybe he just got too much sun. Do you have any water for him?"

"No, his bottle is empty." Sunshine pulled a dusty baby bottle out of the multicolored bag that was slung over her shoulder.

Beth looked around, wondering what to do, and spotted the curtain twitch in a window in the rectory next to the church. Someone must be watching them. "Hang on, I'll go get some water and maybe a cool washcloth to wipe his face."

She took the baby bottle from Sunshine, raced across the parking lot, and knocked on the rectory door. It was immediately opened by a middle-aged, portly priest, only a few inches taller than her, wearing a short-sleeved black shirt and a clerical collar.

He smiled and said, "Oh, hello. You must be the library lady."

"Guilty!" Beth said with a small, forced laugh. "Sorry to bother you."

She introduced herself and held up the bottle while explaining her mission.

"Of course. Come in, won't you? The kitchen is this way." He led her down a short hallway and into a small, neat little kitchen.

A steaming cup of coffee and a sandwich on a plate sat on the small table.

"I'm sorry," Beth said. "Am I interrupting your lunch?"

"Not at all. I was about to eat, but this is more important. By the way, I'm Father Sullivan."

"Pleased to meet you," Beth said and turned toward the sink. She noticed the leggy geranium sitting on the windowsill as she rinsed out the baby's bottle and filled it with water. "I wonder, could I also have a glass of water for the mother and a cloth to wipe the baby's face? They're both hot and dusty. I'm not sure how far she pushed the baby in a stroller. I'll bring the cloth and glass right back."

"Of course." He got a glass out of the cupboard and handed it to her. "I wonder if they walked here from that commune down the road. That *is* quite a ways away—over two miles, I would say."

"Oh? Is there a commune nearby?"

"Yes, they moved in this spring. They've created quite a stir around here, as you can imagine, being new and different.

From what little I've seen of them, they seem like nice enough young people."

So, Sunshine and the baby are members of the commune that Red Cedar complains about, Beth thought. *That means he must live near them.*

Father Sullivan started opening and closing drawers as Beth filled the glass with water. "I'm sure we must have some clean washcloths. I'm just not sure where the housekeeper keeps them. She's not here right now. She only comes in for half a day to make my dinner and clean up after me. That's more help than I need, really. After all, I'm the only one here." After opening several more drawers, he said, "Aha, here we go." He pulled out a cloth and handed it to Beth.

Beth dampened the cloth and filled the glass with water. Then she carried everything back to the bookmobile. While Sunshine gulped down the water, Beth started to wipe the baby's face. This woke him up and he started to cry, showing off his pink gums and two tiny front teeth. Beth shushed him and handed him his bottle. He grabbed it with dimpled fingers and started to suck on it vigorously, moving his feet up and down in appreciation.

When Beth took the washcloth and glass back to the rectory, she found the priest waiting for her inside the partially open door. "Is the baby alright?" he asked. "You should invite the mother to come in and call for a ride home."

"Thank you, Father, but that won't be necessary. I can give them a ride home. I was just about to move on to my next stop. And, dropping them off won't take more than a few extra minutes."

Besides, it will be a chance to get a look at this commune, Beth thought, *and maybe find out a bit about Red Cedar too.*

Beth gave Sunshine time to select books and check them out. She chose several board books for the baby and a reference work on organic gardening for herself. Then, Beth stowed the little wooden step stool that had been sitting outside the van's door, told Sunshine to hang on to the stroller, and they were under way.

"Tell me where to turn," Beth said as they exited the church parking lot and drove toward the grain elevators that sat across the main road, next to the railroad.

"Go north out of town, then turn left at the first intersection," Sunshine said.

"Are you from the commune?" Beth asked.

"Yes. So, you've heard of it?"

"It's something of a novelty around here, I suppose. The priest mentioned it."

"Oh, right. Yeah, I guess we are out of the ordinary," Sunshine said. "Turn right at the next road."

"Are there many people living there?" Beth asked. "I only ask because, if there are, maybe I could arrange to stop there on a regular basis, after my stop in Plato. That would save you a long walk."

"Yeah, there are around six to twelve or so. It varies," Sunshine said.

"I'm not promising anything, of course, but I can ask," Beth said.

"Oh man, that would be totally groovy," Sunshine said.

"By the way, do you happen to have a neighbor named Vern Cedar?"

"I think so. If it's the guy I'm thinking of, he lives just down the road from us. That's his place on the right." Sunshine pointed towards a farmstead.

Beth slowed down to look over the bright white farmhouse at the end of a short driveway that was edged with white painted rocks. It was surrounded by a lush, green lawn, and two big, round grain bins stood next to the red barn.

"Why do you ask? Is he a friend of yours?" Sunshine asked.

"No, I know him." Beth laughed. "Did you know he does a weekly radio show?"

"Does he?" Sunshine asked. "No, I didn't know that. We only listen to music on the radio."

"Actually, Vern invited me and a couple of my friends to be guests on his radio show. I'm trying to decide whether I want to do it or not. What's he like as a neighbor?"

"Kind of uptight," Sunshine said. "He's always coming around with some kind of complaint."

"That's too bad," Beth said.

"Oh, here we are. Turn here," Sunshine said and pointed to a narrow driveway surrounded by straggly trees.

A multicolored, hand-painted sign nailed to a tree read "Mellow Acres." Beth turned into the driveway and bounced down the rutted drive. She noted with relief that the tilted bookshelves kept most of the books from scattering all over the floor of the van, although a few bounced off.

When she parked in front of the farmhouse, a nude young couple, casually holding towels in front of themselves, emerged from the side of the house. Looking in the direction they'd come from, Beth saw a garden hose had been strung up over a tree branch, with a shower nozzle attached to it. The young man went over to the tap on the outside of the house and bent to turn off the water. Beth turned away before seeing more than she cared to see.

Sunshine stood up and collected her things. "Thanks so much for the ride," she said.

"No problem," Beth said as she helped her unload the stroller. "Happy to help. Look for me about this same time next week. But I'll probably park out on the road, next to the mailbox. I don't want to put too much wear and tear on the van's shocks."

"That sounds great. See you then. It's been real." Sunshine waved to Beth and then turned to meet the shirtless young man who was walking towards her.

Beth turned the van around in the circular drive and headed back down the driveway as a few more books rattled off of the shelves and fell to the floor.

"Real, indeed!" she said out loud to herself and chuckled as she bumped along back out to the road.

Chapter 3

July 5, 1969

Beth and Evie sat across the desk from Red Cedar, on either side of Logan. Beth clasped and unclasped her hands, regretting that she'd agreed to do this interview. Red introduced them and then asked Logan to tell him about the Majestic Theater.

"As some of your listeners might know, we've had theaters in Davison City since the early days," Logan said. "The first one was an opera house, built in the 1890s. One big name you will recognize was Mark Twain. He appeared there in 1895 as one stop on his lecture tour of the West. That theater closed in the first decade of the twentieth century. The Majestic Theater was built in 1913. When movies became more popular than plays, the Majestic was remodeled into a movie theater. However, movies on TV, and the competition with movie theaters in Grand Bend that came along with improved roads and faster cars that made it easier for people to go there for a night out, cut into the audience, causing our movie theater to lose business and eventually close."

As Logan continued to talk about the history of the Majestic Theater, Red nodded, smiled, and took notes.

This is going better than I expected, Beth thought. *I thought Red would pepper Logan with interruptions and questions.*

"And you decided to buy the theater and reopen it because . . . ?" Red asked.

"Well, as a drama teacher, I love live theater. And, I knew from my teen years working in the Majestic, when it was a movie theater, that everything from its live-theater days was still there, including the original stage curtain and dressing rooms. So, all we'd have to do is tear down the movie screen, do some cleaning, updating, painting, and *voila*, we'd be good to go."

"That's right. You're a high school drama teacher, aren't you? I noticed some young people helping out when I stopped by last week. Your students, I presume? Are they paid staff, or volunteers?"

"Volunteers. We have a very small staff." Logan laughed. "In fact, the only paid staff member, so far, is our director. Before the first show opens, we'll hire a technical director to handle lights, props, and so on, and someone to supervise wardrobe and makeup. Our first production is *The Importance of Being Earnest*, which will open in September."

"Your director is Nigel Bergenson, is that right?"

Logan nodded, then realized that he was on the radio and leaned toward the microphone and said, "That's right."

"Is he a local guy or an outsider?"

Logan tilted his head, narrowed his eyes, then said, "He's from the Twin Cities—"

Red cut him off. "From the Twin Cities, you say. Is he a good friend of yours?"

"No. As I was saying, he's someone with theater experience and—"

Red interrupted again. "Right, so he's, shall we say, the only one with theater experience involved in this effort?"

Red leaned back in his chair and grinned back at Logan.

"As you know, I have theater experience as a drama teacher," Logan said.

"Right, but not in professional theater. So, would you say this is a risky venture?" Red asked. "It's a good thing you are a single man, so you don't have a family depending on you."

Beth looked from one to the other, as Logan glowered and Red grinned back at him. To break the tension, she leaned toward the microphone and said, "As a member of the public, and as a theatergoer, I'm really looking forward to the opportunity to attend theater in my hometown."

Red looked at her as though he'd forgotten she was there. "Indeed! Listeners, the young lady butting into the conversation is Beth Williams. Logan brought along two female friends to shore him up, so to speak. Tell me, Miss Williams, did you attend much theater while living in the Twin Cities for, what was it, ten years?"

"As a matter of fact, yes, I did."

"Alone or with someone else?"

"It varied." She was starting to feel uneasy about where this was headed.

"It varied. I see." Red drummed his fingers on the desk. "Was one of those varied folks the man you were *dating,* a Dr. Ernest somebody, who later dumped you? Funny, now you're helping out with a play called *The Importance of Being Earnest.* Is that just a coincidence, or are you hoping for a reconciliation?"

"He didn't *dump* me. We decided it was best . . ." She stopped and bit her lip, as she felt her face growing warm. *Damn, I let him get to me*, she thought.

Evie leaned toward the microphone. Her face was flushed and eyebrows scrunched down. "We came here to talk about the theater, not about our personal lives."

"Listeners that is the voice of the lovely Miss Evie Hanson. Tell me, Evie, does your fiancé, who is currently fighting for his country in the jungles of Vietnam, know how you spend your spare time? And who you spend it with?"

"That is a vile insinuation," Logan said.

Red laughed a short, barking laugh. "So says her former boyfriend, as he leaps to her defense. Shall I tell my listeners about certain events you'd rather not share?"

"I don't know what you mean, Vernon. But there are a few interesting things I could say about you too," Logan said.

The conversation went downhill from there, with Red hurling insinuations, and Beth, Evie, and Logan trying to bring the conversation back around to the upcoming theater season.

Finally, Logan had enough and started talking over Red. "We are in the process of auditioning. So, if anyone in your audience wants a chance to act—"

"In a nineteenth century snooze fest," Red interrupted.

"I wouldn't characterize it as such. It is a fast-paced farce—"

"With zero relevance to today's world," Red broke in.

"That's your opinion. Others may think differently," Logan said. "For example, one lady who auditioned for us—"

"You are referring to my wife, I assume," Red said. "She changed her mind and will not be accepting the part."

"Indeed? Well, we haven't completed our auditions. Then, if our director offers her the part, we'll see what *she* says," Logan said.

"I told you what she said," Red said.

Logan clamped his mouth shut, took a deep breath, and glared at Red.

"I think we've said what we came to say. Shall we go?" Logan asked Beth and Evie.

They nodded in agreement.

"Time's up, anyway," Red said and laughed again.

As they left the booth, Beth glanced up at the producer sitting behind a pane of glass. He shrugged apologetically and gave her a small wave. She nodded in his direction.

*   *   *

After the radio interview, Beth, Logan, and Evie stopped by the Pig and Whistle for a much-needed beer. Beth took a sip from her mug and set it down on the wooden table of their booth. Logan stooped over the jukebox in the corner, picking out songs.

Beth said to Evie, "I never got to use the statistics I looked up about the chances of success for new theaters. I had it with me." Beth patted her purse.

"I guess he found better ways to bug us." Evie laughed.

"I have to hand it to him. He knows how to stir things up." Beth sighed and took another sip of beer. "If everyone in town didn't already know about my failed relationship, they know it now. And those insinuations about you and Logan—he really is a low-down skunk!"

"Don't worry about it. If that gets back to Jim, it'll just make him mad at Red. He knows better than to worry about me and Logan."

The opening strains of "Hit the Road Jack" filled the air. Logan came back to the booth and slid in across from Evie and Beth, grinning and singing along with the chorus. Beth and Evie laughed and joined in. After another round and more up-tempo songs, the three of them were laughing about old times and making plans for the theater.

When the song "Let's Twist Again, Like We Did Last Summer" started, Logan said, "Who wants to dance?" He got up and held out his hand to Evie, who was sitting on the outside of the booth.

"I'm not much of a dancer." Evie blushed, suddenly feeling very shy.

"Oh, come on. Don't be a square," Logan said.

"A square? Who are you calling a square? Let's dance. You too," Evie said, motioning to Beth.

"No thanks. I'll sit this one out. You two go ahead," Beth said.

Evie laughed as she got up, and she and Logan danced their way back towards the jukebox.

The screen door banged open and shut. Beth looked up and saw Bill Crample sauntering toward the bar. He noticed Beth, waved to her, changed course, and came over.

"Hi, Beth," Bill said. "Your friends are having a good time." He nodded toward Evie and Logan. "You're not dancing?"

"I'm not much of a twister. Want to join me?" She indicated the bench across from her.

"Okay, but I can't stay long. I just stopped for a quick one before I head home." He slid in across from her.

"Just finished work?"

"Yeah. And I guess you stopped by after your radio interview," Bill said.

"Uh-huh. I gather you heard it." Beth grimaced.

"Yeah, part of it."

"What did you think?"

"That Vern was a jerk. But I suppose you expected that."

Beth shrugged. "Yup. Nothing new there. We figured we'd get a little free PR for the theater."

Logan and Evie came back laughing. Evie flopped down next to Beth, out of breath.

"Hey, look who's here," Logan said to Bill.

"Hi, Logan, Evie." Bill nodded to them. "Okay if I join you?"

"Sure." Logan slid in next to Bill.

"Looks like you two were having fun," Bill said.

"Oh, yeah," Evie panted. "Let me catch my breath. I'm not as young as I used to be."

"Don't say that," Logan said in mock horror. "I'm about the same age as you are. I refuse to think of thirty as too old to have fun."

Beth noticed Bill watching Evie and Logan appraisingly.

Vern's insinuations about Logan and Evie made him wonder. He's probably not the only one who will be watching them and wondering. In fact . . . She stole a long look at Evie. *No. Evie is her normal friendly self, nothing more. But what about Logan?* She watched as he smiled at Evie. *How does he feel about her?* Beth wondered, and then wondered why she cared.

"What were you guys talking about?" Evie asked Beth.

"The interview. Bill caught part of it," Beth said.

"What did you think?" Logan asked.

"Like I just said to Beth, Vern was being his usual jerky self," Bill said.

"That's okay," Logan said. "He didn't get to me."

"Really? I thought you stormed out," Bill said.

"That's because he was being rude to the girls." Logan smiled at Beth and Evie. "Anyway, we were done. We said what we went there to say."

The waitress came over and Bill ordered a beer.

"No big deal," Beth said after the waitress left. "We can handle it. Right, Evie?"

"Yeah. He's not worth a second thought," Evie said.

Logan, Beth, and Evie laughed while Bill looked at them appraisingly. "If you say so," he said.

The waitress came back with Bill's beer, and he finished and then left. The rest of them decided to stay for dinner and ordered hamburgers and fries.

Chapter 4

July 6, 1969

Beth drove the bookmobile down the dusty gravel road, speeding up as she passed Vern Cedar's farm. She hoped he wasn't out in the farmyard. She'd rather he didn't see her. What if she passed him on the road? Should she wave or pretend not to notice him?

The radio interview on Saturday had left a bad taste in her mouth. Sure, she'd laughed it off while she was with her friends. But, being publicly accused of having been dumped after a decade-long relationship had stung.

She noticed two people in his farmyard and was relieved that neither of them was Vern. The woman, a thin brunette wearing jeans and a sleeveless, floral blouse, was laughing and talking to a man.

Looks like Vern's wife, she thought.

The man was facing away from her, so she didn't get a good look at him. There was something familiar about him.

She drove a short distance further to the hippie's farm, Mellow Acres, and parked next to their mailbox, which leaned at an acute angle. It looked like a strong wind would topple it over. She hoped they were expecting her. She tooted the horn a couple times, opened the sliding door on the side of the van, hopped out, and put out a stepstool to make it easier for kids to climb in.

Beth paused to soak in the quiet of the countryside. The only sounds were the west wind ruffling the wheat growing in the field across the road and the flutter of passing swallows as they swooped through the air. The quiet was interrupted by the laughter of children as a bunch of them ran towards her. They were followed by two sleepy-looking young women. One was Sunshine. She was carrying her baby boy in a colorful cloth sling and chatting with the other, darker and plumper young woman, who walked next to her, with her head inclined toward Sunshine as though listening.

"Go ahead. Go inside and pick out some books," she said to the kids as they rushed past her, laughing and talking, and climbed up into the van.

"Hi, Sunshine," Beth said. "I guess you got the postcard I sent you."

"Yeah, we did!" Sunshine smiled radiantly. "It's really groovy of you to go out of your way for us."

"No problem. It's only a few extra minutes for me. It's much easier for me to get here than for all of you to get into town. It looks like there are a bunch of kids here today."

"Yeah, we have a few more people staying with us," Sunshine said. "Some of those kids are Amber's." She nodded towards her friend and introduced Beth. "She's staying with us for the summer. The other kids are from a couple families who are just stopping by for a few days." Sunshine paused, then said, "Oh, I wonder, can those other kids check out books?"

"Yes, if you or Amber are willing to check them out for them. Let's go inside and figure it out."

As Beth turned to climb back in, she noticed holes in the farm's sign. "Oh, no! What happened to your lovely sign? It looks like someone used it for target practice," she said.

A cloud passed over Sunshine's face. "That happened a few nights ago. We didn't see who did it, but we suspect our neighbor."

"You mean Mr. Cedar?" Beth pointed down the road towards his farm.

"Yeah. He seems determined to get rid of us." Sunshine squared her jaw. "But we're not leaving. We have as much of a right to be here as he does." She looked at Beth and then Amber. "Sorry! I didn't mean to bum you out." She laughed a small, self-deprecating laugh. "We don't know for sure it was him."

"Maybe it's just kids goofing around," Amber said.

"Yeah, maybe," Sunshine said, sounding doubtful. "Whoever it is, I worry that a stray bullet might hit a person or an animal. I just hope, whoever it is, they're a good shot."

Amber looked startled, then laughed. "For sure!" she said.

Beth gestured toward the bookmobile. "Come on in and browse."

They got in and Beth followed them, sat down, and swiveled the driver's seat toward the small circulation desk that separated the driver's area from the rest of the interior. She watched, smiling, as the kids pulled books off the shelves and sat down cross-legged on the floor to browse through them.

Sunshine bent over awkwardly to retrieve a book from a bottom shelf, hugging her baby against herself so he wouldn't swing forward as she did so.

"Let me hold him," Beth said, holding out her arms.

"Are you sure?" Sunshine asked, already pulling the sleeping baby free from his cloth hammock.

"Absolutely. I've had lots of experience with babies. Besides babysitting, I helped my mom take care of my little sister when I was a teenager," Beth said.

Sunshine deposited her son into her arms. "I have to admit, it's a relief. That little guy weighs a ton." She put her hands on the small of her back and arched it. "I won't have to haul him around much longer. He's already crawling. I bet he'll be walking soon."

"Silas, right?" Beth asked. "How old is he?"

"He'll be six months old in a few days," Sunshine said.

"So, I guess it'll be a little while yet until he's walking," Beth said. "Which is probably a good thing. Once he's walking, he'll get into everything."

When the kids started piling stacks of books on the circulation table, Beth handed Silas back to his mom and busied herself checking the books out to Amber and Sunshine. The kids were all under school age—too young for their own library cards. Soon, the kids got bored with waiting, jumped out of the bookmobile, and started chasing each other around it.

Beth's concentration was interrupted by the loud honk from a truck horn. She looked through her side window and saw a man in the truck, wearing a Massey Ferguson cap and sunglasses, gesturing angrily toward her. She swiveled sideways and rolled down the window. When he spoke, she realized it was Vern Cedar.

"Keep those kids off the road," he shouted at her.

"What?"

"Those kids." He gestured towards the little kids, who had stopped running and were staring up at him. "They're running in the road. Anyway, what are you doing out here, besides wasting taxpayers' money?"

"Bringing out books, obviously."

"I'll go keep an eye on the kids," Amber said. She got out and started herding the kids off the road and back to the passenger side of the van.

"Who's that? Another squatter?" Vern shouted. Without waiting for an answer, he continued. "I don't have time to slow down for every kid or mongrel mutt I see on the road. From now on, you'd better look out for me, because I won't be looking out for you," he yelled in Amber's direction as she disappeared around the side of the van.

Sunshine flushed angrily. "See what we have to put up with! My boyfriend says that if Vern Cedar hurts one of our kids or dogs, he'll beat the crap out of him! He's not normally violent, but that man brings out the worst in him."

"Hopefully, that doesn't happen. Have you talked to the police about his threats?"

"Oh, no. We wouldn't know who to call. Anyway, we don't have a phone. We used to, but it was a bill we didn't need. We're trying to get back to basics."

"I have a friend who's a cop. Do you want me to ask him what you should do?"

Sunshine looked alarmed. "No. Don't do that. We'll handle it ourselves. Maybe I'll bake some cookies, take them over to his place, and talk it out."

Beth thought that was unlikely to work, but said, "Okay. If you're sure."

"Absolutely. Some of us don't want the cops coming around. We're trying to stay off the grid. You know?"

"Oh, sure. I see," Beth said.

Sunshine glanced at the flyer advertising auditions for the play, which Beth had taped down onto the circulation counter, and then looked at it more closely. "What's this? Are they holding auditions for *The Importance of Being Earnest*? I didn't know there was a theater in Davison City."

"They're opening one in the old movie theater that closed down," Beth said. "Are you interested in auditioning?"

Sunshine beamed at Beth. "It would be so rad! I was in that play in high school." Then her smile faded. "But I don't know if I can. There's Silas to think about and everything. Anyway, how would I get there? Our vehicles are always breaking down."

"Yeah, that's a problem," Beth said. "Wait a second. Your neighbor, Mrs. Cedar, auditioned. If she gets a part, maybe you could ride in with her." She paused, recalling the troubled relationship between the neighbors. "Anyway, if you want to think about it . . ." She dug under the desk, pulled out a flyer, and handed it to Sunshine.

Sunshine perked up again, thanked Beth effusively, and rushed off.

While Beth had stowed everything, she thought things over and decided to stop next door to have a word with Mrs. Cedar before heading to her next destination. If she could encourage Mrs. Cedar to take the part, if offered, that would help Sunshine and Amber too. Vern couldn't have any serious qualms about his wife taking part in a play. Could he?

She glanced in the rearview mirror as she drove off. Sunshine and Amber were looking at the flyer, talking and laughing.

As she approached Vern's farm, she noticed the loud roar of machinery. Vern's truck was parked alongside a grain bin, and a long auger and spout was pulling grain out of the bin and pouring it into the back of the truck. He was nowhere in sight. The man and woman she'd seen earlier were nowhere in sight either.

Beth pulled into the driveway and parked while looking over her shoulder and glancing in the rearview mirror, hoping to have a quick word with Mrs. Cedar while avoiding Vern.

Beth knocked on the door. Mrs. Cedar opened it. She wore a frilly apron over her blouse and pedal-pushers and was wiping batter off of her hands. Her overplucked eyebrows rose in surprise when she saw Beth.

Beth introduced herself. "I'm sorry to bother you, Mrs. Cedar. I was just next door with the bookmobile." She gestured toward it.

"Oh, sure, you're the new librarian. Come on in. And, please, call me Ruth."

"Thank you, Ruth. But I can't stay. I just wanted to stop by and introduce myself. I saw you when you auditioned at the theater the other day."

"Oh?" Ruth looked confused. "Were you there auditioning too?"

"No. I was painting. I'm a volunteer."

"Okay, well, what can I help you with? I'm right in the middle of making some bread. So, I really can't stand here and chat. So, if you would come in."

"Oh, sure." Beth walked into the kitchen and watched as Ruth resumed kneading a pile of bread dough resting on her kitchen counter. "As I said, I just wanted to introduce myself and say that I hope you will get the part that you auditioned for. You see, the girls next door—"

"The hippies?"

"Yes, the hippies. Anyway, one of them, a young mother named Sunshine, was hoping to audition too. She's had experience in the theater. But she says she has transportation difficulties, and she also mentioned that she doesn't have a phone. So, if you could bring her along, it would be great."

"I don't know. Vern's kind of against it."

"Really? Why's that?" Beth said, trying to sound as though she knew nothing about it.

"Who knows? He likes to keep me under his watchful eye." Ruth punched the dough.

"I see. Well, I don't want to get between the two of you. That's all I came to say. I should get back to work."

Vern slammed through the door. "You! What are you doing here?"

"I just stopped by to say hi to your wife. I'm going now." Beth started inching toward the door.

"She's here about the theater," Ruth said. "She wants me to take the part, if it's offered."

"We talked about this," Red said. Turning to Beth, he said, "She's too busy. She has other things to do."

"You said," Ruth said. "But I didn't say. If I want to get out of the house now and then, I'll do it. I'm not your prisoner."

Vern's face turned a darker shade of crimson as he clamped his mouth shut and stalked out of the room.

"He'll calm down. You'll see. By opening night, it will have all been his idea, and he'll be glad-handing everyone in sight. Leave it to me." Ruth smiled cryptically as she massaged the dough.

Chapter 5

July 13, 1969

Beth plopped down on her beach towel spread out next to Evie's, who was lying face up on her beach towel, her long blonde hair twisted into a knot on top of her head and her eyes hidden behind sunglasses. Beth pulled off her swim cap, got a bottle of pop out of the cooler at her feet, and opened it with the bottle opener that was tied to the cooler's handle.

"Aren't you even going in for a dip?" Beth asked.

"Maybe later." Evie adjusted her sunglasses and then yawned. "I'm trying to get a tan."

"Fat chance! With your fair skin, you'll just burn."

"Not this time. I'm using special tanning oil."

"Right!" Beth snorted derisively.

Evie turned on to her side to face Beth and propped her head up on her fist. "How's the water?"

"Perfect. Just right for a brisk swim," Beth said.

"In other words, cold," Evie said.

Beth laughed. "Well, it's not bathwater warm. But, it's still nice. Isn't it great to be outside on this glorious Sunday afternoon? Not indoors, painting the theater."

"About that . . ."

Beth groaned. "Oh no! Don't tell me. More painting?"

"Yup. Did I tell you? Logan offered to pay me for scene design."

"He did? When did this happen?"

"Last weekend. I was telling him about my stagecraft class that I took last year, and he offered me a part-time job."

"That is so exciting! Why didn't you tell me?"

"I wasn't sure I wanted to take it. I already have a job in the art restoration store."

"Yeah, but that's only part-time too. Couldn't you do both?"

"I could. But I also have the summer photography class, and I don't want to be too busy. After all, this is my last summer as a carefree single gal. I want to enjoy it."

"So, have you and Jim set a date for the wedding?"

"Not an exact date, but we're talking about around Christmastime. He'll be home from the army, and the church will be all decorated. It should be ideal."

"That sounds perfect. I'm so happy for you."

"Thanks," Evie said and then sighed.

"What? You don't sound too excited."

"It's just such a long time off, and we've been engaged for years now. Most of the kids we went to high school with are married with kids, houses, the whole works. Something always seems to come up to postpone our wedding. I guess I don't dare to get too excited about it yet."

"It'll be fine. You'll see. You're not getting cold feet, are you?"

"Me? No way. I can't wait to be Mrs. Jim Vincent."

"Glad to hear it." Beth wondered if Evie really was eager or was just trying to convince herself. Maybe there *was* a spark developing between Evie and Logan. "Anyway, are you going to do both jobs or what?"

"No, I already handed in my notice at the art store. I asked the owner if I could work flexible hours around the theater gig, but she said no. Apparently, she has a niece who wants to work in the store. Of the two jobs, I'd much rather do set design. It'll be more fun and be more creative. Plus, and here's the best part, I asked Logan if you could work with me and get paid, and he said sure!"

"Really? I thought he was nearly broke—but, maybe he's not. Get paid, huh? Well, I can always use a few more bucks. How many hours are we talking about?"

"Not many. Logan may not be broke, but he's not exactly loaded. If he was, he wouldn't be hiring someone like me, with no experience and very little training. I'll work half-time up to opening night. You have your regular library job, so maybe just a few hours on Saturdays. You'll have to work out the details with Logan."

"Okay, I'll give him a call. When did you think that I would start?"

"Next weekend, if you're willing. I thought we'd paint some scenery."

"Aha! So, it is more painting."

"But painting scenery, not walls. Come on. It'll be fun." Evie smiled encouragingly.

"Scenery? What kind of scenery?"

"I was thinking of doing a garden for the outdoor scenes. The indoor scenes are mostly just props, I think. I haven't worked it all out yet."

"You know I'm artistically challenged. Anything I painted would look like a little kid did it."

"No, it won't. I'll draw the outlines and tell you what color goes where. Then, it's just like a paint-by-number picture. Some of Logan's students will help too. And—"

"Okay, okay. I can see you're determined to talk me into this. I'll do it, on one condition."

"What's that?"

"That you stop talking about it and swim a couple of laps with me."

"You sure like to swim. You know I'm not as strong of a swimmer as you are."

"I don't know why not. We both took lessons at the pool when we were kids," Beth said.

"Yeah, but I haven't done much swimming since."

"That's okay. It'll come back to you. It's like riding a bike." Beth examined her tall, thin friend. "I'll admit, that when it comes to swimming, I have an advantage." She patted her tummy. "My size sixteen body comes with built in flotation devices." She jumped up and started pulling Evie to her feet. "Come on. Let's go."

After a little more encouragement, Evie got up and reluctantly tiptoed into the water, hesitating and letting out little shrieks with every step. But soon, they were splashing their way back and forth across the swimming area.

Later that day, Beth's phone rang. She dropped the TV dinner she'd been unwrapping on her kitchen counter and grabbed the receiver of the black wall phone.

"Hello."

"Beth, it's me," Evie said in a breathless voice. "Turn on the channel five news."

"Why? What's happened?"

"It's about Red—Red Cedar. Quick! Before you miss it. Then call me back."

"Okay."

Beth hung up, rushed into the living room, and switched on the set while trying to imagine what kind of stunt Red had pulled to get himself on the evening news. By the time the TV warmed up, the story had nearly ended. A somber-faced newsman was standing in what appeared to be a farmstead, with the flashing lights of emergency vehicles lined up behind him.

"All we know at this time is that local farmer and radio show host Mr. Vernon Cedar has died in what appears to be a tragic accident. Now, back to you, Ed."

"Wow," Beth said to her cat, Chestnut, who had followed her into the living room, meowing to remind her that she was late getting his supper. "Wow!" Beth said again. "Yeah, meow, meow, I got it. Just a sec. I'll get you your din-dins."

Beth rushed back into the kitchen, quickly poured out his kibbles, and tossed her TV dinner in the preheating oven before calling Evie back.

"Hi, it's me."

"Did you see it?" Evie asked.

"I only caught the last few minutes. What happened?"

"Red Cedar died in an accident."

"Yeah, I got that part. What kind of an accident? When did it happen?"

"It was a grain bin accident."

"A grain bin accident? What's that?"

"For instance, maybe he got buried by grain in his grain bin."

"You're kidding! I've never heard of such a thing."

"Really? It's fairly common. Happened to one of my dad's cousins. As I understand it, grain is kind of like quicksand. It can seem solid and then suddenly collapse in on you, and you can't break free."

"No kidding? That's awful. Did it just happen?"

"That's the thing, they don't know exactly when it happened. His wife had been away from home for a couple of days. When she came home, Red wasn't around. She didn't think anything of it at first, but after a while she started to wonder, because both his car and truck where there, and she started looking for him. By the time she found him, he'd been dead for some time."

Chapter 6

July 19, 1969

Beth examined the large canvas drop cloth spread out on the floor backstage, which was being transformed into a garden. Once finished, it would be stapled onto wooden supports and become the backdrop for the outdoor scene. Evie had applied a coat of base paint and sketched the outline of flowers, bushes, and a path against a background of trees.

Beth decided where to start, poured some red paint into a cup, took it and a brush, and knelt down on the edge of the canvas. She dipped the brush in the paint and began to fill in outlined red petals and then swore under her breath as red paint spattered onto the already painted green leaves.

This is not as easy as Evie said it would be!

She retrieved a wet rag from the worktable and began to clean up the splatters. She heard the footsteps and voices of two people as they crossed the stage. They paused on the other side of the curtain. Beth recognized Logan's voice.

"As far as I'm concerned, good riddance!" he said.

A low woman's voice said something that she couldn't make out.

"So, I went out there. So what?" Logan said.

Then, they started walking again.

What were they talking about, and who was with Logan? Beth wondered. She tiptoed to the side of the curtain and peeked out in time to see Logan's back as he disappeared behind the curtain on the other side of the stage. She paused, wondering if she should follow him.

Evie's voice startled her. "Beth, where are you?"

Beth turned toward her. "Here I am."

"Oh, hi. How's it going? Is the paint the right consistency?"

Beth held up the rag she was carrying and joined Evie at the workbench. "It's a little thin. I had a problem with spatter."

"So, you gave up?"

Beth laughed. "No, that's not it. I heard Logan talking to someone, and I wanted to see who she was."

"She? So, it was a woman. What were they talking about? It must have been something interesting."

"I'm not sure. Logan said something was a 'good riddance' and that it didn't matter if he was out there, wherever *there* was. I couldn't make out what the other person said, but it was a woman's voice."

"That *is* interesting. Do you think they might have been talking about Vern Cedar's death? Everybody's been talking about that, and Logan wasn't exactly broken up about the accident," Evie said.

"Could be, I suppose."

"Do you think the woman could have been Vern's wife, Ruth?"

"Unlikely. Like I said, I didn't see her. But Logan wouldn't say 'good riddance' about Vern to Ruth. Would he? That's not like him. Maybe it was the wardrobe lady."

"Jessie? Yeah, it could have been. Although, I haven't seen her around here today. The only people I know are here, besides us, are a few student volunteers who are building set frames in the basement work area. But Logan probably wouldn't say anything like that to one of them either. Who else is around?"

"Nobody, as far as I know. But, let's keep an eye out," Beth said. "Meanwhile, try this paint and see what you think. Maybe it's just me."

Evie took the cup of paint and brush, crouched down over the canvas, and deftly filled in a few red petals.

"It could be a little thicker, I suppose. I'll use this batch and make up some thicker paint for you to use on the garden path. I want that to look a little rough, anyway. I'll be right back." Evie started to leave.

"Just a sec. While you're gone, I'm going to look around and see if I spot our mysterious female. Keep an eye out for her downstairs too," Beth said.

"Okay." Evie gave her a thumbs up, then left.

Beth went through the curtain, crossed the stage, and headed in the direction Logan had disappeared. She walked down a hallway, passing dusty old props, boxes, sandbags, and other debris, and down a short stairway to the side door. She pushed the door open and glanced up and down the alley. No one was in sight. She retraced her footsteps back to the stage, then went down the stairs into the auditorium, up the aisle, and through the swinging doors out into the lobby.

Beth stopped short. Logan was near the ticket booth talking to Officer Bill Crample. They fell silent when she stepped through the door and turned in her direction. Bill was wearing his "cop face," a studied, neutral expression. Logan looked angry and confused.

"Yes, Beth, what is it?" Logan asked.

"Um, I . . . that is, I thought I heard you talking to Evie. Have you seen her?"

"No." Logan looked around distractedly. "Isn't she backstage with you or downstairs?"

"I'll–I'll go see," Beth stammered. "It looks like you're busy." She turned toward Bill and nodded. "Hi, Bill."

He just nodded to her.

"Um, Beth, I'm going to the police station," Logan said. "Tell Evie to lock up when she goes, if I'm not back by then."

Beth felt a bubble of alarm rise in her throat. "What do you mean, if you're not back? Why wouldn't you be back?" She looked from Bill to Logan and then back again.

"He's just helping us answer some questions we have," Bill said while examining the tips of his shoes. "It shouldn't take too long," he said to Logan.

"Questions about what?" Beth asked. "You mean questions about Vern's death? I thought that was an accident."

"That's none of your business," Bill said.

Beth stared at them, open-mouthed, trying to make sense of everything. Her mind raced. *So, the police must think Vern's death was suspicious. Why? And do they think Logan might know something about it? Does he? No, that would be crazy!*

"Let's go," Bill said to Logan.

"So, you'll tell Evie what I said?" Logan asked Beth.

"Sure, yeah, of course," she said.

Logan squared his shoulders and walked out of the theater, followed by Bill Crample.

Chapter 7

July 22, 1969

Beth ran up the front stairs of the library and burst in, with a few minutes to spare before her shift started. As usual, Miss Tanner was sitting at the circulation desk. She looked over the top of her tortoiseshell glasses at the clock, and then at Beth, and then removed her glasses and let them dangle from the beaded chain around her neck.

"Good afternoon, Beth. Running late today?"

There was a slight stress on the word "today" with the implication that this was not an unusual occurrence, which, Beth thought, was a pretty valid insinuation. She tucked the pencil she'd been using into her dyed-red beehive hair and gathered up the catalogs and correspondence spread out on the desk.

Beth paused long enough to say, "Sorry, Miss Tanner. I lost track of the time."

Beth rushed past the circulation desk, through the nonfiction stacks, and into Miss Tanner's office. There, she stashed her purse and lunch bag into the top drawer of a filing cabinet which served as her locker. She then peeked in the mirror on the wall and readjusted the wide paisley headband that kept her light-brown hair somewhat under control and then rushed back out to the circulation desk.

"Well, I'm sure you have a lot on your mind," Miss Tanner said. "It's so unfortunate that the young Mr. Rusk was arrested. I imagine that will delay the theater opening. I heard him speak about his plans for it at a fundraiser earlier this year. He was most enthusiastic."

"It's all a big misunderstanding, and it will soon be cleared up," Beth said.

"Indeed?" Miss Turner arched her plucked and painted eyebrows. "What makes you think that?"

"It's just ridiculous to think that Logan, that is, Mr. Rusk, is responsible for Vern's death."

"I see." Miss Tanner examined Beth for a moment. "Well, do try to stay out of trouble this time. Leave investigating to the police. We don't want you falling into the river again, or anything like that."

"No. That is, yes. I will try to stay out of trouble, and I will certainly not fall into the river. Not that I ever did fall into it, I just pulled someone out of it, and—"

Miss Tanner cut her off. "Yes, I know. It was just my little joke. Anyway, I'm leaving a couple catalogs for you to browse through. Mark the pages and items if you see anything you'd like to add to your special collection. Well, I must dash."

Beth had no idea what Miss Tanner rushed off to do every evening. She was very tight-lipped about her personal life. She lived alone with not so much as a pet to take care of. Beth thought she probably just liked to maintain an air of mystery.

After Miss Tanner left, Beth took a turn around the floor, picking up books off of tables and the ends of shelves and placing them on a book cart for reshelving. Then, she went to the periodical room to straighten the magazines and newspapers. The front-page section of the local newspaper, *The Daily News*, was lying on a reading table. The headline read, "Local Man a Suspect in Suspicious Death of Radio Personality."

Beth read the article before placing the stick back on the newspaper display stand. It didn't tell her anything she didn't already know, just that Vern's wife had returned home and found him dead in his grain bin. As for why they considered it a suspicious death, rather than an accident, the article didn't say.

Beth sighed. This really *could* delay the theater opening, which would probably sink the whole enterprise if, as rumor had it, Logan had put in everything he had and borrowed heavily to finance the theater.

There must be something Evie and I could do! We solved a couple of murders; maybe we can solve this one too. But what if they solved it, and it turned out Logan did it? The thought gave her pause. Beth shook her head. *No, I'm sure he's innocent.*

But, she reminded herself, she'd just assured Miss Tanner that she'd stay out of trouble.

She's right. I should let the police investigate. I bet they'll soon realize they made a mistake. Anyway, I'm a librarian, or I will be once I complete my MLS, not a private eye. I need to concentrate on finishing my degree and starting my career.

Beth marched back to the circulation desk and turned her attention to the book reviews. But she found she couldn't concentrate. She kept picturing Logan being marched out of the theater, followed by Officer Bill Crample.

Feeling restless, Beth got up and started reshelving books, a task usually left for the high school library volunteers. *At least if I do it, I won't have to undo all of their mistakes*, she thought as she rearranged books in the 300 section of the Dewey Decimal System. It was a big section, and the volunteers only seemed to pay attention to the first three numbers, not those after the decimal.

The bell on the circulation desk rang, breaking her concentration. She turned to see Mr. Nobis, a lawyer and a member of the Friends of the Library group. He was wearing a dark suit, highly shined shoes, and a dazzling smile on his abnormally tan face.

She smiled back, raised an arm in greeting, and hurried over to the desk while wondering what brought him to the library. This was the first time she had seen him here, except for Friends of the Library events.

"Hello, Mr. Nobis. How can I help you?"

"Call me Fred." He widened his smile.

Why was he being so friendly? What does he want?

"Okay, how can I help you, Fred?" That sounded weird to her.

"I thought I'd just pop in and say hello and tell you that Logan is okay. I understand you are a friend."

"Yes, we are. Thanks for letting me know. That's good to hear." She hesitated. "So, does that mean you're his lawyer?"

"I am."

"Why did they arrest him? He's not guilty, you know. When will he be released?"

Mr. Nobis held up a hand to stop her. "I can't say more at this time. Lawyer-client privilege."

"Of course," Beth said.

Mr. Nobis continued to smile at her expectantly.

"Was there something else I could help you with?" she asked.

"Mrs. Cedar mentioned that you are bringing books to the farm that is next door to her place. Is that correct?"

"Yes, that's right."

"I just wondered if you ever noticed anyone around the Cedar place—a stranger, perhaps."

"No, not that I can recall," Beth said. "Of course, I've only driven past their place a few times and didn't always notice what was going on there. But, no, I don't recall seeing any strange cars or . . ."

She hesitated, remembering the man she'd seen talking to Ruth as she drove past. But surely Ruth would have mentioned him to Mr. Nobis, if he was worth mentioning. Probably just the hired hand. The phone rang in the librarian's office.

"I need to get that," Beth said.

"Okay. Call me if you remember anything," Mr. Nobis said and turned to go.

Beth raced to answer the phone. When she picked it up, she was surprised to hear Evie's voice on the other end.

"Oh, it's you. Hi, Evie."

"Sorry to bother you at work."

"No problem. It's pretty quiet right now. I was just out reshelving books and then talking to Mr. Nobis."

"Mr. Nobis, the lawyer?"

"Yup, that's the one."

"What did he want?"

"I guess he's sort of investigating." Beth recounted what he'd asked her. "How about you? What's up?"

"I'm at the theater. Can you stop by on your way home?"

"I guess so, but that'll be pretty late. Will you still be there?"

"Yeah, we're all feeling kind of at loose ends and trying to figure out what to do next. I suggested waiting and talking to you too."

"What are you figuring out?"

"What to do about the theater since Logan's arrest. Like, if we should delay our opening."

"Who all is there?"

"Besides me, Nigel, and Art and Jessie Hanson, the couple that Logan hired to handle the lights and wardrobe. And, since you're working here too—"

"Well, hardly, just a few hours a week."

"Still, I want you to be part of the conversation. And . . ." Evie hesitated. "They kind of wanted to call you. Can you come?"

"Yeah, of course, but why me?"

Evie hemmed and hawed a bit, then said, "They want us to investigate."

"Really?" Beth wasn't sure if the flutter in her stomach was from excitement or nervousness. "Why's that?"

"I don't know. It was Jessie's idea first. She's a seamstress and helps out with costumes for school plays, and so on, on the side. That's how she knows Logan."

"And she thinks—what?"

"She talks to a lot of people. I'll bet the other cases we worked on were a big topic of conversation. So, now, she thinks we can find the real killer and clear Logan."

"I see. Well, what do you think? Is it something you want to do?"

"I guess we should try. After all, I'm sure he's innocent. And, I did quit my job to work here. It'd be a shame if the theater goes under before it even starts, and I'm out of a job. Not that that is the most important thing. The main thing is clearing Logan. The sooner we figure out who really did it, the better."

Beth hesitated. "Well, I'm not sure. But we can talk about it."

"Great! You close at eight, right?"

"Yup, see you shortly thereafter."

Beth began clearing the last few library patrons out at fifteen minutes to eight, locked the doors on the dot at eight, and hurried to the theater.

Chapter 8

July 22, 1969

Beth got to the theater a few minutes after closing the library and found Evie waiting for her in the lobby. She let Beth in and locked the door behind her.

"Come on, everyone's backstage," she said.

Evie preceded Beth through the auditorium, across the stage, and backstage to the breakroom area, where three people sat, looking like birds on a wire, at a folding table waiting for them. Beth knew Nigel but not the middle-aged couple sitting next to him.

They all stared anxiously as Beth and Evie approached. Beth felt her chest tighten and bit the bottom corner of her lip. She'd mulled over what she could say or do that would help ever since Evie's phone call but hadn't come to any conclusions. She said "hi" to everyone, nodded to Mr. and Mrs. Hanson as Evie introduced them, and then sat down across the table from Mrs. Hanson. Evie sat down next to her.

"Well, here we are. The whole crew." Evie smiled and looked expectantly at Nigel.

He took the hint. "As I said earlier, I think we have to remain hopeful that all of this . . ." He waved his hand in a circular motion. "This unpleasantness will be sorted out. Meanwhile, I propose that we continue to plan for opening night, as announced. If things don't work out . . ." He paused. "That is, if it takes longer than expected to sort things out, well, we'll cross that bridge when we come to it. Agreed?"

Everyone looked at each other nervously before nodding and mumbling in agreement.

"Okay, but how will we function?" Art Hanson asked. "Who's in charge, now that Logan is gone? Temporarily gone, we hope," he asked Nigel.

"I guess I'm in charge. As the director and stage manager, I'll get on with auditions, rehearsals, and everything. As for paying the bills, the paychecks and so on, I'll do the best I can. Hopefully, Logan will be back with us shortly."

"Speaking of getting Logan back . . ." Jessie Hanson leaned towards Beth. Her heavily made-up face thrust forward under a pile of improbably dark curls. "I think everyone in town knows about you two." She nodded toward Beth and Evie. "Can't you do something?"

"Do something?" Beth echoed. "Like what?"

"You know, investigate," Jessie said.

"I don't know. I haven't really thought about it," Beth said cautiously. "Have you, Evie?"

"A bit, but I wouldn't even know where to begin," Evie said.

"I gather that you two have some experience investigating crimes, and Jessie thinks you might be able to prove Logan's innocence. Is that right?" Nigel said.

"Beth and Evie are famous in Davison City for solving mysteries," Jessie said.

Beth smiled. "Well, that's an exaggeration. Evie and I helped the police solve a couple of cases recently. We're not actual detectives."

"All the same . . ." Jessie paused and looked to her husband for help.

He harrumphed a couple of times and adjusted his wire-rim glasses. "My wife and I discussed this last night, and she thought, that is, we thought you two ladies could assist the police in clearing this up quickly. If you could, it would be a blessing. We all agree, I think, that Logan had nothing to do with Vern's death." He looked around at heads nodding in agreement. "I'm sure it was just an unfortunate accident. The police must have it all wrong."

Beth noticed all eyes on her. Art and Jessie looked hopeful. Nigel looked skeptical. Evie looked worried.

"I see," Beth said. "You're kind of putting me on the spot." She chewed her bottom lip nervously and glanced sideways at Evie. "Of course, I also think that Logan is innocent and that it's just a matter of time until the police realize it too."

"Does that mean you'll investigate?" Jessie asked.

"Evie and I will talk it over and then decide what to do," Beth said. "If we think we can help, then, yes, we'll investigate. But, even if we do, there are no guarantees we'll find out anything useful. That's all I can say for now."

"Oh, good! As long as you try," Jessie said with a sigh of relief. "I'm sure you'll crack the case. After all, we need Logan back for opening night."

No pressure, Beth thought. *I just hope we find out that he's really innocent.*

After the meeting broke up, Evie drove Beth home and came inside for the offered cup of tea. Now, they sat on opposite ends of the couch cradling mugs of tea. An open package of sandwich cookies lay on the coffee table in front of them. Chestnut purred between them, happy to be surrounded by his favorite humans.

"So, what do you think?" Evie asked Beth for the second time. "How should we begin?"

Beth stared into her mug as if searching it for inspiration. "I wish I had a clue. I suppose Logan is suspected because he threatened Vern. But there must be more to it than that. Given how obnoxious Vern was, he must have received death threats on a regular basis. If only we could talk to Logan, maybe he could tell us more. But I suppose that won't happen until he's out on bail."

"Do they release murder suspects on bail?" Evie asked.

"That's a good question. We could start by finding out. I guess I could ask Mr. Nobis. Or Fred, as he asked me to call him." Beth smiled and batted her eyes suggestively.

Evie raised her eyebrows. "He did? When did this happen?"

"When he came into the library today."

"It sounds like he's sweet on you."

"I feel so special." Beth chuckled. "Actually, I feel like one of many. I hear he's been on the prowl since his wife dumped him."

"All the same, he'll probably like chatting with you. Find out if, and when, Logan will be bailed out."

"I'll give it a try."

"Meanwhile, I'll take a look around Logan's office in the theater and see what I can turn up."

"Good idea," Beth said. "I don't have to go to work tomorrow. I guess I'll take a drive out to the Cedar farm and see what Mrs. Cedar can tell me."

"How about the hippies? You should visit them, too, while you're out that way. One of them might have seen something."

"Another good idea," Beth said. "Hey, look at us. We have a bunch of leads already."

"What about Bill? Are you going to talk to him?"

"Eventually." Beth leaned forward and took another sandwich cookie. "But I know what he'll say: 'Don't get involved. Leave it to the police.'" She munched on her cookie. "I think I'll wait until we have something to go on before I talk to him."

"Yeah, that makes sense." Evie took another cookie, too, and examined it for a moment. "So much for my diet."

"You don't need to diet."

"I do, if I want to fit into my wedding dress."

"At Christmastime, right?"

"I hope so. Jim says the war should be over by then."

"Really? That would be great. It would be such a nice time for a wedding. The church will already be decorated."

"As long as the weather cooperates. I don't want people sliding into ditches to attend our wedding."

They discussed the pros and cons of winter weddings and made plans to get together again tomorrow evening to compare notes on their sleuthing.

Chapter 9

July 23, 1969

The next morning, Beth drove north along the highway that ran parallel to the railroad tracks that went to Canada. Fields of waving grain and knee-high sugar beets stretched out in all directions under the blue dome of the sky. In the distance, here and there, clumps of trees indicated farmsteads in the otherwise treeless landscape.

Nothing to see and nothing to get in the way of seeing it, Beth thought. *Or, as Dad would say, "big sky country."*

Just before she got to Plato, Beth turned left onto a gravel road heading west and then right on another one. Soon, she arrived and pulled into the driveway of the Cedar farmstead. A bubble of anxiety rose in her chest as she searched for signs of the alleged crime, but everything looked perfectly ordinary—no crime tape or other evidence of police activity was in sight.

She parked and started walking toward the house. A curtain twitched, and a few moments later Ruth Cedar opened the door and stood there, arms crossed and eyes squinting suspiciously.

Beth raised a hand in greeting and called out, "Hi, Ruth. It's Beth—Beth Williams. How are you?"

After a pause, she responded, "Oh, yeah. You drive the bookmobile. Right?"

"That's right. I just stopped by to see how you're doing. I hope that's okay."

Ruth sighed. "Sure. I suppose you'd better come inside."

She held the screen door open and gestured Beth to come in.

Beth stepped past her into the porch and then followed her into the kitchen.

"Have a seat." Ruth pointed to the kitchen table.

Beth sat down and accepted the coffee that Ruth offered her. Soon, they were sitting across from each other. Beth tried to make small talk about the weather, but Ruth just sat and stared out of the window. Beth paused, and they sat in silence for a few moments.

Ruth looked at Beth and smiled weakly. "Sorry, I'm just a little distracted."

"No, that's okay. It's perfectly understandable."

"It's just kind of hard to get used to. I went out of town for a few days, and when I came back, everything had changed."

"I'm sorry for your loss."

"Thanks." Ruth shook her head. "It's no secret that we weren't on the best of terms lately. But I assumed there was time to make it better. And then . . ." She lifted a hand and let it fall with a slap onto the table. "Time's up. It's just so sudden."

"I'm sure it must have been a shock," Beth said. "So, you were away when Vern died?"

"Yes. I went to the cities to do some shopping. I go several times a year to shop at Dayton's, Donaldson's, and other stores we don't have closer to home. Well, you know. I understand that you used to live there."

"Yes, I did. Although, I mostly only window-shopped in those stores. Mine has always been more of a Penney's and Sears kind of budget."

Ruth ran a critical eye over Beth's outfit, a peasant blouse, cut-off jeans, and flip-flops.

"Well, I like to pick up one or two better pieces, when I can. Not that there are many reasons to dress up around here." She sighed. "I was hoping that after the new theater opened, there might be some parties, or who knows what. But I suppose that won't happen now."

"Oh, I don't know. We met last night and decided to go ahead with opening night as planned, if possible."

"Really? Who decided that?"

"Nigel and the rest of the theater crew."

"And you were there, at the meeting? I thought you were just a volunteer."

"Yup, I was there. Logan hired Evie to be in charge of props and scenery, and me to help her, for a few hours a week."

Suddenly, Ruth became more alert and smiled. "Oh, I see. More coffee? How about a cookie?"

"Thank you, that would be lovely."

While Ruth bustled around the kitchen, she asked, "Do you know if they've made any casting decisions yet?"

Beth suppressed a smile at Ruth's change in demeanor. *So much for the grieving widow routine*, she thought.

"I don't think so. Are you still interested? I can let Nigel know, if you are. Of course, everyone would understand if you want to withdraw, under the circumstances."

"Oh, I'm still interested. It's best to keep busy. Don't you think?"

"Yes, I'm sure you're right. Of course, everything is a bit tentative at the moment." Beth paused and took a sip of coffee. "Did you know that Logan was arrested? Or, taken in for questioning, anyway."

"Yes, I heard that. But I'm sure it was just an accident. Vern was always messing around with his equipment, and he wasn't very careful. I half expected something like this to happen eventually. You know what I mean? Farming is so dangerous. You always hear about some kind of accident, don't you?"

"Absolutely. Why do you suppose the police think it wasn't just an accident?"

"I have no idea. They didn't say."

"But they questioned you, right? What kinds of questions did they ask?"

Ruth crinkled her forehead in concentration. "Mostly about time. Like, when did I leave, and when did I get back? When did I discover the body? That sort of thing."

"And what did you say?"

Ruth looked at Beth appraisingly. "Why all these questions? What's going on? The police are already investigating."

"Yes, I'm sure they are. It's just that the others at the theater seem to think that Evie and I can help get to the bottom of things. If we prove that Logan had nothing to do with Vern's death, that it was just an accident, then things can get back to normal. That's what we all want. Isn't it?"

"I suppose so." Ruth pursed her lips in thought. "That's right. I recall hearing something about how you two solved a case."

"Well, we helped solve it," Beth said. "And, maybe we can help again."

"Okay. I guess it can't hurt. I left on Friday afternoon, spent Saturday shopping, and drove back on Sunday. When I got here, Vern wasn't around. I didn't think anything of it, until later when I was making dinner and still hadn't seen him. That's when I went out there."

"And you found him then?"

"Yeah." The color left Ruth's face. "I–I don't want to think about that."

"Sorry. It must have been bad." Beth didn't say anything more for a few moments. "And that's when you called the police?"

"Yes." Ruth's voice was husky with emotion.

"Sorry to make you go through all of this again," Beth said. "I think I'll get going. But, before I leave, do you mind if I have a look around? Not that I expect to find anything. I'm sure the police went over everything. I didn't see any police tape, so I guess they must be done here."

"No, I don't mind."

Beth started to leave, then stopped, her hand on the doorknob. "By the way, where did you stay?"

"What do you mean?"

"In the cities, on Friday and Saturday night. Where did you stay?"

"Oh." Ruth paused. "At the downtown Radison, in Minneapolis. I always stay there when I go shopping. It seems so long ago now."

Ruth pointed out the grain bin where she'd found Vern's body. Beth made a beeline for the bin. She hauled herself up onto the metal step that was under the door and started wrestling with the outer door. She leaned sideways while trying to latch it back out of the way, but the wind kept pushing it back towards her before she could hook it.

A short middle-aged man wearing dirt-encrusted coveralls appeared outside of one of the storage buildings and sauntered up to her.

"What is it that you're trying to do, Miss?" he asked and smiled, showing off uneven, stained teeth.

"Oh, hello, Mr. er . . ."

"Just call me Dave," he said, touching the brim of his dusty green cap.

"Okay, Dave. Mrs. Cedar said I could look around, and I'm trying to get a look inside of this grain bin, but I'm having a little trouble latching this door back."

"Here, let me do it," he said.

Beth jumped down. Dave hopped up, leaned over, hooked the outer door back, and then undid the latch on the inner door. He hopped back down and gestured for Beth to climb up.

"All set. But, there's nothing to see. I cleaned it out after the police had a look."

Beth leaned into the dark, hot interior. A large sweeping auger and a thin scattering of wheat grains on the floor was all she saw. The interior smelled faintly of bleach.

She hopped back down. "So, this is where Mr. Cedar was found?"

"Yup, or so I'm told. I didn't find him."

"Why's that? Didn't you wonder why you hadn't seen Mr. Cedar?"

"Nope. I wasn't here. I was working at another farm when he disappeared."

"Oh, I see. Which farm was that?"

He hitched a thumb back over his shoulder. "At the Olson's place, up the road."

"You said you cleaned out the bin. Did you use bleach? I noticed a faint odor."

"Yeah." He grimaced. "Vern had been there a while, you know, and there was some dried blood. So, I cleaned that up."

"Sounds like a good idea. So, was there a pool of blood or what?"

"More like a streak, like he'd been dragged. Maybe his clothes got caught up in the sweeping auger or something." He paused, and his eyes crinkled in suspicion. "Say, why all the questions?"

"I'm just checking things out."

"Checking things out, huh? Like a detective or something?" His expression changed from suspicion to skepticism. "What did you say your name was?"

"I'm sorry. I guess I didn't say. I'm Beth Williams."

He scratched the stubble under his chin. "Oh, yeah. I heard about you. You're one of those girl detectives they wrote about in the paper last spring, aren't you?"

Beth took a breath, then decided not to try to explain. "Yup, that's me. So, you were gone at the time of Mr. Cedar's death, and so was Mrs. Cedar. Who would have known that?"

Dave looked up at the sky, as though searching it for the answer. "Could have been most anyone, I suppose. The Olsons knew I wasn't here, of course, and anyone who saw me at their place. Not sure about Mrs. Cedar. I suppose someone might have seen her driving off."

He gestured toward the grain bin. "You done here? I better close her up. We don't want to get birds inside. They'd make quite a mess."

"Yup, I'm done. Like you said, nothing to see here."

Dave closed and fastened the doors.

"I'll just poke around a bit more, if you don't mind," Beth said.

"Makes no difference to me." He shrugged.

"Did Mr. Cedar have an office in one of these buildings, where he kept papers and things? Or was that all in the house?"

"I think he kept some ledgers and stuff over there." Dave pointed to one of the outbuildings. "Want me to show you?"

"That's okay. I don't want to take up any more of your time. It's probably all a wild goose chase, anyway."

Beth raised a hand to wave goodbye and headed towards the metal building Dave had indicated, relieved to leave him behind. She didn't want him hovering around, asking questions.

The hinges creaked as she stepped inside. It was considerably warmer inside because of the summer sun beating down on the steel building. It smelled of motor oil and dust.

Farm machines took up most of the space. Off to her right, under a window, a battered wooden desk was covered with dusty stacks of paper, notebooks, folders, and clipboards. A dirty cup, smudged with oily fingerprints, sat on the window ledge. Beth began to sort through the mess and uncovered a desk calendar bearing a seed company logo, the kind that was attached to a ring binder stand, with large squares for notes.

She took a closer look; there were a lot of notes. Most of them were prices. It looked like Vern had been tracking how much he could get for his grain. Looking back, there was a price increase shortly before she'd encountered him on the road outside of the hippies' farm. That made sense; he must have decided the time was right to sell. There were a few other notes, names, and initials. On the Friday, the weekend that he died, there was a note: "R. 4:30." *That must have been when Ruth left for the cities*, Beth thought.

None of the notes seemed to be about his radio show. He must have kept that information somewhere else, maybe in the house. She'd ask Ruth. It could be that someone he'd antagonized on his show had killed him.

Beth flipped ahead and saw that a thinner smattering of notes continued onto the next months' pages. *Poor Vern, he'd been busy planning a future he'd wouldn't have. I guess we never know when our time is up. Do we?* The thought gave her an unexpected pang of sympathy. Vern had been a jerk, but he had been full of life, plans, and energy that had been snuffed out prematurely.

Beth pulled a Brownie camera out of her purse, congratulating herself on coming prepared to document any clues she found. She turned on the desk light, positioned the calendar under it, and took snapshots of the pages. She hoped there was enough light and that the focus was good.

Then, Beth went back to the house and knocked on the door, waited, and knocked again. Still no answer. Ruth must be home. Her car was still in the driveway. She must be asleep, on the phone, or she simply didn't want to talk anymore. Beth shrugged and headed back to her car. She'd talk to Ruth later. It was time to see what the hippies might know.

Chapter 10

July 23, 1969

As soon as Beth turned into the hippies' rutted driveway, a stream of children and dogs rushed towards her. She slowed to a crawl, while nervously scanning the road in front of her, and inched forward. She rolled down her widow and yelled out, "Stay away from the car!"

This had no effect on the kids and just made the dogs bark more wildly.

As soon as the driveway widened into the weedy, packed dirt area in front of the house, Beth pulled over and parked the car. She was a little nervous about the dogs and hesitated before stepping out, but their wagging tails seemed to indicate they were friendly.

"Are your mommy or daddy home?" she asked the closest moppet, a little girl about five years old. Barefoot, she wore just a homemade shift. She had wild blonde hair and a runny nose, and she stared at Beth with round, blue eyes. Beth thought she looked familiar. She was probably one of the kids who'd checked books out of the bookmobile. Was she one of Amber's kids?

"You're the library lady," the little girl said, pointing at Beth.

"That's right. My name is Beth. What's your name?"

"Jemma. She's the library lady!" she announced to her friends, who crowded around, all talking at once, asking her questions and telling her their names.

Beth held a finger up to her lips and gave a loud librarian "shh." They all fell silent for a moment, and she said, "Jemma, can you tell your mommy or daddy that I'd like to talk to them?"

"Okay," Jemma grabbed hold of Beth's hand and pulled her towards the house. The rest of the kids trailed behind. Jemma led her up the wooden steps, onto an open front porch very much in need of paint. The dogs seemed to have lost interest and ran off to find squirrels or rabbits.

Jemma opened the torn screen door and yelled, "Mommy, the library lady wants to talk to you. Mommy! Mommy!"

A bleary-eyed young man stumbled toward the door barefoot, wearing bell-bottom jeans and a vest over his bare chest. His long hair flopped over his eyes, and he brushed it back with one hand.

"Stop yelling, Jemma. Your mommy isn't here. She's out in the garden," he said.

"Oh, okay. I'll go get her," Jemma said and scampered away, followed by the other kids.

Seeming to notice Beth for the first time, he said, "Oh, hey. How's it going? You looking for Jemma's mom?"

"Yeah. Or another adult I can talk to," Beth said.

He paused and seemed to try to focus. "I'm an adult. Or so I've been told. You can talk to me." He looked her up and down appraisingly. "What can I do for you?" He lowered his voice, and it assumed what he seemed to think was a sexy vibe.

"I'm looking into what happened to your neighbor, Vern Cedar. Do you know anything about that?"

He straightened up and seemed to sober up suddenly. "You a cop or something?"

"Me, a cop? No. I'm the library lady, as the kids call me. My name is Beth Williams."

Sunshine drifted around the corner. "Oh, hi, Beth."

"You know her?" he asked.

"Yeah, sure, she drives the bookmobile. Remember? I told you about her. She's okay. Beth, this is my old man, Lester. Come on in."

Beth followed her into the living room, where an assortment of young men and women lounged on beanbag chairs on the floor and on a futon that was folded up and propped up against the wall. They were in the process of passing around a joint, and the young man who currently held it offered Beth a hit.

"No thanks." She waved it away.

"Most of these are friends who are staying with us for a few days. Everyone, this is Beth," Sunshine said.

They smiled and mumbled greetings.

"So, they weren't here when Vern died?" Beth said.

All heads swiveled in her direction. The guy on the edge of the futon, who had been handing the joint to the girl next to him, paused mid-motion. "What's that?" he asked. "Who died?"

"Nothing to worry about, just a neighbor who died recently," Sunshine answered. "No, the only ones around then were me, Lester, Amber, and her old man, Greg. That's him, over there."

She pointed to a young man with thinning hair sitting cross-legged on the floor. He raised a hand in acknowledgement.

"Maybe we could hang out in the kitchen," Sunshine said. "I was grinding some wheat to make bread."

"Sure," Beth said.

Sunshine led the way, and Beth followed. A few moments later, Lester and Greg trailed in behind them. Beth returned to the wheat grinder, which was clamped onto the table. Beth and the two men sat down on mismatched wooden chairs arrayed around the large wooden table which took up most of the room in the kitchen. Sunshine scooped a cup of grain out of a plastic bucket, dumped it into the hopper of the grinder, and cranked the handle. A thin stream of coarse ground flour fell into a large bowl set under the spout.

"That smells wonderful," Beth said, "but it looks like hard work."

"I don't mind. It's my meditation," Sunshine said. "We don't have electricity right now, and it takes a lot of bread to feed all of us. Sometimes I get help."

Beth thought she heard a thinly veiled complaint that her "meditation" was wearing thin, and she could use a bit more help.

"I suppose you're all wondering why I'm here," Beth said. "A friend of mine, Logan—you know, the theater owner—was arrested for killing Vern, and I'm sure he didn't do it. I'm trying to set the record straight."

Sunshine stopped grinding and sat down. "I thought it was an accident."

"Maybe it was," Beth said. "But the police don't seem to think so. My friends at the theater asked me and my friend Evie to see if we can figure out what really happened. I was just over at the Cedar farm. I talked to Ruth and the hired hand, Dave. They both said they were away when Vern died. I wondered if anyone here noticed anything odd that happened around that time."

"When was that?" Lester asked.

"About the eleventh through the thirteenth," Beth said.

They looked at each other.

"Of course, we noticed all the commotion from the police cars and news crews that Sunday," Lester said, "but nothing before that."

"We wouldn't be likely to see anything," Sunshine said. "Our house is set back from the road, and we're surrounded by trees."

Amber came in looking windblown and sunburned, lugging a large wicker basket brimming with oversized zucchinis and other vegetables which she deposited on the table. Everyone stopped to ooh and ahh over the harvest.

"Wow, you must have a big garden!" Beth said.

"Oh, hi, Beth. The kids told me you were here. Are our books overdue?"

Beth laughed. "No, that's not why I came."

"Yeah, the garden is pretty big," Amber said as she sorted through the basket, making piles of various vegetables and depositing them on the sink's drainboard. "But I guess I really overplanted the zucchinis. I had no idea how many we'd get off a dozen plants. I can't keep up with them! I guess we'll have a big veggie stir-fry over rice for supper tonight. And, look, the first of the ripe tomatoes." She held one up for another round of praise.

Amber washed her hands, splashed water on her face, and toweled off with a dingy-looking towel. Then she ran a glass of water and sat down with it at the table.

"The kids said you wanted to talk to me," Amber said to Beth. "If it's not about overdue books, then what?"

"She's investigating Vern Cedar's murder," Greg said.

"What?" Amber's head swiveled toward Greg and then snapped back toward Beth.

Beth repeated what she'd told the others, then asked, "So, did you notice anything out of the ordinary?"

"I was just telling Beth that we couldn't see anything from the house," Sunshine said.

"No, I suppose not." Amber stopped and drank down her glass of water and got another one. "Except, I can kind of see their place from the garden."

"You can?" Beth asked.

"Yeah, it's back behind the woods to get good afternoon light, and there's nothing but a wheat field between our garden and the Cedar house."

"Oh, that's right," Sunshine said.

"I remember hearing some machine noise from there on Friday night," Amber said. "I was out there after supper, tying up tomato plants. I was trying to tell you and the kids to be careful not to tie them too tightly, and there was that background noise. Remember that, Greg?"

"That's right," he said. "I remember that, now that you mention it. And that's weird, if no one was around."

"That is odd," Beth said. "I suppose they might have left something running by mistake. What kind of sound was it?"

"It was a constant sort of rumbling, kind of like when they fill the grain trucks," Amber said.

She looked at Greg for confirmation, and he nodded.

"Did you notice when it stopped?" Beth asked.

Everyone looked around and shrugged, shook their heads, or said "no."

Beth asked a few more questions but didn't elicit any further information, and the subject shifted to plans for dinner. Sunshine and Amber urged Beth to stay and eat with them, but Beth had other ideas. A hamburger and French fries sounded more enticing that a veggie stir-fry. Maybe Evie would be up for comparing notes at the Big Boy tonight.

Chapter 11

July 23, 1969

Beth an Evie were sitting in their favorite booth at the back of the Big Boy restaurant. Beth salted her French fries, dipped one in ketchup, and tasted it. It was hot, crispy, and delicious. She tried not to smile too broadly across the table at Evie, who was nibbling on a salad, dipping each forkful gingerly into the dressing she'd asked to have served on the side.

"Have you heard of zucchini bread?" Beth asked.

"Sure, my mom makes it. Apparently, it's all the rage. She and her friends are passing around recipes for it. Why do you ask?"

"My hippie friends handed me a big bagful before I left this afternoon, and I'm not sure what to do with it. Do you want to give it to your mom?"

"I'll take a couple, if you have extra. Maybe you should share some with your mom. I bet she makes zucchini bread too."

"Yeah, but she probably can't use a whole bagful. Apparently, zucchini grows in great abundance. The hippies practically held me hostage until I agreed to take some with me." Beth laughed.

"How did the farm visits go, outside of the unwanted produce?" Evie asked. "How's Ruth doing?"

"She's okay. I got the impression she's not exactly grief-stricken. She seems pretty interested in whether she will get a part in the play."

Beth relayed what else had happened and what she'd learned.

She concluded, "The one thing that stood out was the noise coming from the Cedar farm on Friday evening. According to Amber and her husband, Greg, they heard it after Ruth and Dave, the hired hand, said they were gone. So, who turned on the machinery, or whatever it was, that was making the noise?"

"Maybe it was Vern."

Beth stared. "Of course!" She struck her forehead. "It could have been him. Why didn't I think of that!"

"Right. We really don't know when or how he died. Do we?" Evie said.

"No. Just that they found him on Sunday in the grain bin and that it seemed like he'd been caught in the sweeping auger." Beth repeated what the hired hand had said about the blood in the bin. "I assumed that he was in the grain bin on Friday evening, and then someone turned on the auger. But, you're right, he could have turned it on himself. Anyway, from what I saw, it's not like the auger would have killed him, because it doesn't spin around superfast. A person can just step over it," Beth said. "So why is it that people die in grain bin accidents?"

"I think there are a couple reasons for that. When there's more grain in the bin, people walk around on top of it, hit an air pocket under the surface, break through, sink into it, and can't move because it's so heavy," Evie said. "Sometimes they just suffocate from the weight of the grain, or their clothes get tangled up in the auger and they're pulled under. Or when there's less grain, like when they're cleaning out the bin, they trip, or their clothes get snagged by the sweep auger, with nasty consequences."

"Oh man, that sounds gruesome," Beth said.

"Yeah, it is. But, in this case, the grain bin was empty. Right?"

"Yup. It was empty when I saw it." Beth took a bite of her hamburger and chewed thoughtfully. "Here's a thought. Maybe Vern emptied out the grain bin on Friday night, and that was the sound the hippies heard. In that case, there's some grain sitting around on the Cedar farm, waiting to be sold, because Vern didn't have a chance to take it to the elevator. Or, he was still alive on Saturday morning, and he *did* take it to the elevator. Either way, that should help narrow down the time of death."

"You didn't see any grain sitting in a truck, did you?"

"No, but the hired hand might have moved it to one of the sheds. I didn't look in all of them."

"But if that's the case, wouldn't the hired hand have mentioned it?"

"Unless he didn't want me to know for some reason or just didn't think to mention it."

Evie reached across the table and hovered her hand over Beth's plate. "Can I have one of your fries? Not that I should."

"Go ahead. One French fry won't make you fat," Beth said.

"Stop me before I eat them all," Evie said and popped one into her mouth.

"Just try to get another one." Beth pretended to guard her French fries.

"So, here's the question, did Vern go to the grain elevator on Saturday morning, or not?" Beth said. "If not, is there a wagon full of grain sitting in one of the sheds?"

"Maybe the police already know the answer to that. I wish we could find out what they discovered. Do you think Bill would tell us?" Evie said.

"Unlikely. I suppose I could ask him. He usually stops at the bar for beer after work. Should we try to catch him?"

"It's worth a try," Evie said. "Also, Ruth found the body and called the police. Right? Maybe she saw something that she hasn't mentioned yet. Should we talk to her again?"

"Sure, if we get a chance," Beth said.

"What about the hired hand; did he have an alibi?" Evie asked.

"Sort of. He said he was working at the Olson farm down the road. But even if he was, he might have come back to the Cedar place at any time before, after, or during his workday. I don't imagine anyone was keeping a close eye on him," Beth said.

"Any reason he might have wanted to kill Vern?" Evie asked.

"Not that I know of. Of course, like most people, he probably didn't like Vern. But he seemed perfectly okay letting me look around, like he had nothing to hide. Speaking of which, while I was poking around, I found a cryptic note on the calendar on Vern's desk in one of the outbuildings. There was a letter R and the time 4:30 on Friday the eleventh. I took a picture of it with my camera."

"Really? That's very Nancy Drew-ish of you. Say, I can develop those pictures for you. I have access to a dark room. You can't exactly drop off the film at the local drugstore, unless you want everyone in town to know about it."

"Great! I was hoping you could. Otherwise, I'd probably have to send it through the mail or drive back and forth to Fargo to get them developed anonymously."

"No problem. I could use the practice," Evie said. "What do you think the R on the calendar meant?"

"I don't know. It could have just meant that was when Ruth was leaving on Friday. Come to think of it, when I asked Ruth when she left for the cities, she just said 'Friday afternoon.' We should ask her about that," Beth said. "Did you discover anything today?"

"Not really. I searched Logan's office, but I wasn't sure what to look for. I looked at his calendar—nothing suspicious there. I looked through his Rolodex. I noticed that he has Vern's home address, which is probably not suspicious. He probably planned to contact Ruth about her audition."

"That's true. Did you look inside the desk?"

"Just a bit. He's kind of a pack rat. It was a jumble of pens, pencils, old letters, pictures—old pictures of the theater, and of him and his wife—even a bird feather and a broken watch, all sorts of stuff. You'd think he'd been there for years. I suppose you didn't get a chance to talk to Logan's lawyer yet."

"Nope. That's a job for another day," Evie said. "Say, I wonder if he wants any zucchini."

They both laughed.

Chapter 12

July 23, 1969

Beth and Evie stopped by the Pig and Whistle after supper. Bill was sitting at the bar, nursing a beer. He looked up as they came in and nodded hello. They went over to join him.

"Hi, how's it going?" Beth said.

"Can't complain. What have you two been up to?"

"Not much," Beth said. "We had supper at the Big Boy and thought we'd drop in for a beer before heading home. Oh, and trying to give away zucchini. Do you want some?"

"Zucchini? What's that?" Bill asked.

"Summer squash. People make bread with it too—kind of like banana bread, only green. It's all the rage amongst home bakers."

"I don't know about that. Why do you have so much?"

"Her hippie friends gave it to her," Evie said.

"So, you've been out that way. You didn't happen to stop at Ruth Cedar's place?"

"I might have," Beth said. "Just to say hello."

"And snoop around too. Right?"

"I wouldn't call it snooping. But, yes, I did look around," Beth said. "How did you know?"

"I didn't. I just suspected as much."

"To be fair, we were asked to look into things," Evie said.

"By who?" Bill asked.

"The rest of the theater staff," Evie said.

"Is that so? And why is that?" Bill asked.

"Obviously, they think we're some kind of dynamic duo and that we can help clear Logan, so we can get on with putting on a play," Beth said.

"Obviously," Bill said. "And none of you think the police can handle it."

"I wouldn't say that. I think they just hoped to speed things along," Beth said. "I don't know if we can, or if we're just duplicating your efforts. Would it be possible to ask you a few questions?"

The bartender took Beth and Evie's order, poured, and served their drinks.

Bill sighed. "I suppose there's no point in telling you to stay out of it."

"Not really, no. Sorry," Beth said.

"Okay, you can ask. I don't know if I'll answer," Bill said. "Shall we take a booth?"

He indicated a booth across the room. They went over and sat down, Bill on one side, Beth and Evie sat across from him.

"So, what can you tell us about the investigation?" Beth asked.

"What do you want to know?"

"How about the body? Ruth said she found Vern in the grain bin. What can you tell us about that? Do you have any idea how he died or when?"

"Yes, he was found in the grain bin. As far as the approximate time of death or the cause, the medical examiner hasn't released that information."

"Wasn't the cause pretty obvious?" Evie asked. "Wasn't he entangled in the sweep auger?"

"That's a reasonable assumption, I suppose," Bill said.

"But, not the case?" Beth asked.

Bill looked at her sharply. "No. But keep that quiet."

They promised.

"It looked like the machinery got hold of his coveralls and pulled them off. When they got entangled in the gear, a belt snapped, and the blades stopped rotating."

"That's interesting," Evie said. "So, if someone else was there, they didn't hang around and watch, or they would have realized that."

"But, why assume that someone *was* there?" Beth asked. "Evie and I were talking about it over dinner and wondered, where's the grain?"

"The grain? What grain?" Bill asked.

"The last load of grain. Suppose Vern was sweeping out the grain bin, and he switched on the auger himself. Then, there should be some grain waiting to be hauled. Either that, or he hauled it away on Saturday. If we can discover that he was alive and hauling grain on Saturday, that would narrow down the time of death."

"No, that's not what happened. We checked," Bill said. "The hired hand swept out the bin after it was empty and before he left for the Olsons' farm. Vern hauled the last of the grain to the elevator on Friday afternoon, except for a few bags he kept, I suppose for animal feed."

"So, we're back to square one," Evie said. "He could have died any time from when the hired hand last saw Vern on Friday to when Ruth discovered the body on Sunday."

The door opened, letting in a blast of hot and humid summer air along with a tall, stocky man. Beth thought he looked familiar, but she couldn't place him.

"Who's that?" Beth asked Evie, nodding in his direction.

"That's Don Winthrop," Evie said. "Remember him? He's a couple years older than us. He used to be a big football star for Central High School."

"Oh, yeah. And now?" Beth asked.

"He sells advertising for the radio station," Evie said.

"Oh, really?" Beth watched with interest as he walked over to the bar and ordered a drink.

Don seemed to sense that he was being watched, turned, and raised a hand in greeting. Once he had his drink, he carried it over to their booth.

"Hi there," Don said and smiled a brilliant smile with what seemed like too many teeth. "I know Evie and Bill, of course, but who is this charming young lady?"

"This is Beth Williams," Evie said. "We went to school together. Beth, this is Don Winthrop."

"Oh sure, of course. You're the famous librarian slash detective, aren't you?" He flashed another vivid smile and held out a hand, which Beth shook.

Beth laughed a small, self-deprecating laugh. "Just a librarian in training, actually."

"That's not what I hear. I hear that you're not just finding books for people. The word is, you're currently looking into Red Cedar's death. Is that right?"

Bill had been glaring at Don with thinly-veiled irritation. He got up and said, "I have to go. See you later, ladies, Don."

"Mind if I join you?" Don asked and slid into Bill's vacated spot without waiting for an answer.

"Are you interested in the investigation of Red Cedar's death?" Beth asked.

"Of course. Everyone is, especially at the radio station," he said.

"Sure, I suppose you knew him well," Beth said.

"Well, enough." He pulled a face. "Not to speak ill of the dead, but, well, you know."

"I gather he had more enemies than friends," Beth said.

"You could say that," Don said.

"Was there anyone in particular who held a grudge against him?" Beth asked.

Don wrinkled his brow and took a sip of his whiskey. "Nobody I can think of. No one at the radio station, if that's what you mean. His show was controversial, but it was popular. It was growing our audience. He'll be missed."

"What about any of the people he ragged on?" Evie asked. "Did the radio station get any calls from outraged individuals?"

Don shrugged. "I suppose. But I haven't heard of anyone in particular. Maybe the station manager would know."

"Can you ask and let us know?" Evie asked.

"Sure. If I do, does that make me part of your gang?"

Beth hesitated. "Well, I don't know . . ."

Don laughed. "Just kidding. Sure, I'll see what I can find out. I'll pop by the library and let you know. When do you work?" he asked Beth.

"Tuesday and Thursday afternoon and evening," Beth said.

"Great, see you soon," Don said.

Beth and Evie finished their beers, while Don talked about plans for the town's Pioneer's Day festival. As soon as they could get a word in edgewise, they excused themselves and headed out.

"You have an admirer," Evie said as they headed toward their parked cars.

"What? Who?"

"Oh, please. Don, obviously."

"No way!" Beth laughed. "Don? He's not my type."

"Oh, I know. But you seem to be his type."

"Do you think so?" Beth thought about it for a few moments. "Well, if so, I hope it motivates him to actually follow through, check with the station manager, and get back to us. And when he does, I'll ask if they have recordings of Vern's show and if we can listen to them. Then, we'll see if anything jumps out."

"Don't you think the police will do that?" Evie asked.

"Are you kidding? I doubt they have the manpower for that," Beth said. "Anyway, it's worth asking." They arrived at their cars. "See you tomorrow?"

"Yup. See you then," Evie said.

Chapter 13

July 27, 1969

It was Sunday evening, and Beth was ensconced on her couch, ready for an evening of mindless TV, when she heard a knock on her door. She reluctantly dislodged Chestnut, who was purring on top of her, and answered the door.

To her surprise, it was Bill in his police uniform.

"Oh, hi, Bill. What brings you here?"

"I just got an assignment, and I thought you might be interested."

"Sorry, I'm not sure what you mean."

"I'll tell you all about it. Mind if I come in?"

"Not at all." She stepped aside and waved him in. "How about a cup of coffee or something?"

"No thanks, I can't stay. I just had an idea and wanted to talk to you about it."

"Okay." *He's being cryptic*, she thought. "Well, take a seat."

Bill sat down next to Chestnut, who curled up next to him. Beth switched off the TV set and sat down on the chair across from Bill and waited.

After some hemming and hawing and a few false starts, Bill said, "I'm supposed to go out to the Cedar farm to pick up some evidence, and I wondered if you wanted to come too. That is, as long as you stay quiet and just observe. Not in the squad car, of course, but separately."

Beth stared at him in amazement. "Is that kosher?"

"Well . . . maybe not. But if you just happened to be there, I don't see the harm."

"What kind of evidence?"

"As I understand it, the hired hand was taking apart the gearbox of the floor auger and managed to untangle the coveralls that Vern was wearing when he died."

Beth sat up straighter and leaned forward. "Really?"

"Of course, it may not tell us anything we don't already know."

"True." She stared at Bill suspiciously. "What's going on? Why are you suddenly including me?"

He laughed uneasily. "I figure you'll butt in, no matter I say, so I might as well invite you along and keep an eye on you. Who knows? Maybe you'll spot something I miss. So, are you coming, or what?" He stood up and started for the door.

"You mean, now?"

"Yup. I'm heading out. If you want to go, meet me out there."

"Okay. Do you mind if I ask Evie?"

He half turned, his hand on the doorknob. "Nope. I figured you would."

As soon as Bill left, Beth called Evie and told her what happened, and she jumped at the chance to go along. A short time later, Beth picked her up, and they headed out of town.

Beth pulled into the driveway of the Cedar farm, parked behind Bill's squad car, and she and Evie got out. The sun was low behind the barn and the grain bin. It was getting cooler, and a light west wind fanned the grain in the fields.

Bill was standing in front of the house, talking to Ruth. Dave was crossing the yard, heading toward them. Beth and Evie joined the group.

"Hi, Beth, Evie." Ruth smiled. Her smile didn't reach her eyes.

They said hello to her and Bill.

The dark rings under Ruth's eyes looked puffy, as though she'd been crying. But her hair was perfectly arranged in an elaborate mound on top of her head, and her clothes were perfectly clean. *She couldn't have been doing much outside today while wearing those strappy sandals*, Beth thought, noticing her pink toenails.

"Do you know Dave?" Bill asked Beth and Evie.

"I do," Beth said. "Hello, Dave."

Evie shook her head. "No."

"Dave is the hired hand," Bill said. "He found the evidence that I came to collect."

"Dave, this is Evie Hanson, a friend of Beth's. They're looking into the circumstances surrounding Vern's death. As I explained to Ruth, I asked them to join me."

"Yeah, okay." Dave shrugged. "I already talked to Beth some," Dave said. "I'll show you what I found. Follow me."

"I don't want to see it, if you don't mind," Ruth said to Bill.

"Sure, I understand. That's okay," he said.

"Then I'll be in the house. Come talk to me later, if you need to." She turned and went inside.

The others followed Dave, who was heading towards a storage building.

Bill walked alongside Beth and Evie. He said quietly, "Remember, I'll do most of the talking. I'll let you know if it's okay to ask questions."

They nodded in agreement.

The sliding metal doors of the shed were partly open. It was still warmer inside than it was outside from the midday heat. The air smelled of motor oil and dust. Dave led them over to a cluttered worktable along the side of the building. Various sizes of drive belts hung on the wall next to the worktable, which was strewn with machine parts. Beth assumed they were from the gearbox. Next to those was a desk lamp and a tattered pair of grease-streaked coveralls.

Dave stood a couple feet back from the workbench and pointed at the coveralls. "That there is why I called you," he said to Bill. "I 'spose they got ripped off Vern, got tangled up in the gears, then the belt snapped and the auger stopped. Good thing, or it would have been worse. Well, worse for us. I guess it couldn't have been much worse for Vern. He . . ." He trailed off and glanced at Beth and Evie.

"Yup." Bill picked up the coveralls and held them up at arm's length. One of the shoulder straps and the rivets and hooks used for fastening the straps had been ripped off. The rest of the garment was in one piece but badly torn. Bill put the coveralls back onto the workbench. "Let's see what he had in his pockets," he said.

Beth and Evie stepped forward and stood next to Bill as he extracted a broken comb, a handkerchief, a crushed red feather, and a small, folded piece of paper. Bill unfolded the paper and held it under the desk lamp.

Written in pencil, in large letters, it read, "I know what you did. I'll make you pay." He turned toward Dave and held out the note and shook it. "What do you know about this?"

"Me? Nothing. Not a thing," Dave said.

"Did you write it?" Bill asked.

"No! Of course not! Why would I?"

"And you have no idea who might have written it?" Bill asked.

"No."

"Do you recognize the handwriting?" Bill handed the note to Dave.

Dave took the note and stared at it. "No, I don't think so."

Bill held out his hand, and Dave gave the note back to him.

"You're certain?" Bill asked.

"No. I don't recognize it," Dave said.

"Do you think it might be Vern's handwriting?" Bill asked.

"It sure doesn't look like it," Dave said.

"Okay, then. That's all for now. Do you girls have any questions for Dave?" Bill said.

"Well, I was wondering, when did you last see Vern?" Beth asked.

"Um, I think it was on Friday afternoon. Yeah, I finished cleaning out the grain bin, and then I went to find him. He was at his desk, over there." He gestured toward the machine shed where Vern's desk was located. "He was writing something down. I think he just got back from hauling the last load of grain to the elevator, so maybe he was writing down what he got for it. That's what he usually did."

"What time was that?" Beth asked.

"I don't know. Around five or five-fifteen."

"How did he seem?" Beth asked.

"Pretty regular, I guess. I told him I was heading out. He asked if I'd finished cleaning out the grain bin. I said yeah. That was about all."

"And had he seemed upset about anything lately?"

Dave considered. "No. He was always kind of grumpy, but no more than usual."

"How about you, Evie? Do you have any questions?" Bill asked.

"I'm just wondering about the feather. Why do you suppose Vern had that in his pocket?" Evie asked Dave.

Dave smiled a little, seeming to find it an odd question. "I don't know. Maybe he just thought it was pretty. We don't get a lot of red birds out here. Mostly we just see barn swallows and such."

"Okay, thanks, Dave." Bill took a large evidence bag out of his pocket and shoved the coveralls into it. Then, he put the other things, except the note, into another small evidence bag. We'll get out of your way now."

Bill hung onto the note. He noticed Beth watching him and said, "I'm going to ask Ruth if she recognizes the handwriting."

Bill headed toward the house, followed by Beth and Evie. "Let me do the talking," he said. He stopped at the squad car and dropped the evidence bags on the passenger seat. Bill knocked on the door, and Ruth quickly opened it.

Beth thought she seemed a little annoyed to see Beth and Evie were still there. But she invited them to sit at the kitchen table and lit a cigarette. From the pile of cigarette butts in the ashtray, it looked like she'd been chain-smoking. Bill shoved the note across the table, and Ruth picked it up. Her eyes widened as she read it.

"Where did you find this?" she asked.

"It was in one of the pockets of the coveralls he was wearing when he died," Bill said. "Have you seen this before?"

"No, never! What is it, a threat?" A hysterical note crept into her voice.

"It seems so," Bill said. "Any idea what it means? Was Vern being threatened by someone?"

She tapped the ash off her cigarette into the ashtray. "He didn't tell me everything. He liked having his little secrets." A slight sneer played across her face. "I bet it was one of those kooks he had on his radio show."

Beth glanced at Evie and raised her eyebrows. Evie repressed a smile. Did Ruth know that they had been on Vern's radio show? Beth wondered.

"Had any of the kooks, as you call them, threatened him before?" Bill asked.

Ruth shrugged in irritation. "Not really threats, just dirty looks around town and people that hung up the phone when I answered. He didn't care. He thought it was all a big joke. I told him it wouldn't be so funny if someone punched him in the face."

"Do you recall the names of any of the people who gave you those dirty looks?" Bill asked.

"No." She crushed out her cigarette, spilling some of the cigarette butts onto the table. She shoved the note back towards Bill. "Anything else?"

"Just one question," Beth asked, with a quick glance at Bill, who glared at her. "Do you recall approximately when you left for the cities?"

Ruth looked at her, as though surprised to see that Beth was still there. "When? Um, just after lunch on Friday, I think. I always leave about that time when I go to the cities. I like to get there before dinnertime."

"Okay, Beth and Evie, it's time for you to go," Bill said.

"But, we—" Beth started.

Bill interrupted her. "I said, it's time to go. I have some more questions for Ruth, and I don't want to be interrupted."

"Okay, we're going," Beth said.

Outside, Beth stalked back to her car, got in on the driver's side, and slammed the door shut.

Evie got in on the other side. "He was kind of a jerk, wasn't he?" she said.

"I don't know what his problem is," Beth said. "It was a perfectly obvious question. I don't know why he didn't ask it."

"For sure." Evie hesitated. "Unless he had some plan in mind, like he already knew what time she left, but he wanted to trip her up or something."

"I suppose." Beth felt her irritation ebbing. "Let's just get out of here," she said as she started the car and drove off.

Chapter 14

July 27-28, 1969

The sun was setting as Beth and Evie drove back to Davison City. An orange and golden glow spread across the western rim of the sky, turning the waving grain a dark shade of auburn.

Beth missed the vibrant play of colors. She stared straight ahead at the road and silently fumed about Bill kicking them out of Ruth's house. After a while, she sighed, shook her head, and asked, "What was it that you wondered about the feather?"

"The feather . . . oh, yeah. Just that it was kind of like the one I found in Logan's desk at the theater," Evie said.

"Oh, that's right. You mentioned seeing a feather there. Are you sure it was the same kind?"

"No, I'm not sure at all. I didn't get a close look at the one that was in the pocket of the coveralls. Besides, it was broken. But I thought they looked similar. They were both red, at any rate."

"Why didn't you say anything about it to Bill?" Beth asked.

"I guess I wasn't sure it was relevant. And I didn't really get a chance."

Beth glanced sharply at Evie. "I guess we wouldn't want to call attention to any connection between Logan and Vern if we're not sure it's relevant. Maybe we should stop by the theater before we go home, and look at that feather."

"Maybe we should," Evie said.

"Can we get in?"

"Yup, I've got the key to the theater on my keychain." Evie patted her pocket.

They drove in silence while they listened to "Bad Moon Rising" on the radio and then sang along with the chorus of "Sweet Caroline" and laughed at how off-key they were.

"Feeling better?" Evie asked when the song ended.

"Yeah." Beth sighed. "Bill really bugs me sometimes. He can be such a jerk."

"Be nice," Evie said. "After all, he invited us to come along, and we did learn a few things."

"I guess you're right. We found out when Ruth and Dave last saw Vern alive. And that note was very interesting, wasn't it?"

"I'll say! 'I know what you did. I'll make you pay.' How dramatic! Now, if we could just figure out who was threatening who," Evie said.

"Maybe Vern wrote it and hadn't delivered it yet," Beth said.

"Maybe. But both Dave and Ruth said it wasn't his handwriting," Evie said. "So, it seems like it was from someone who was threatening Vern. I wonder who, and what he did to them."

"He probably ticked off lots of people with his radio show," Beth said. "We'll learn more if we get to listen to the recordings of his shows. I wonder what they meant by, 'I'll make you pay.' Do you suppose someone was blackmailing him?"

"Could be. But then why did he end up dead? A dead man can't pay," Evie said.

"Maybe he refused to pay."

They pulled up in front of the theater and walked down the alley to the side door. Evie unlocked the door and flipped on the hall light. Inside, the still, humid air smelled of drying paint. They walked through the dark auditorium and into the lobby, lit only by the outside street lights.

"Should we turn on a light?" Evie whispered.

"Why are we whispering?" Beth whispered. She giggled, then said a bit louder, "Wait until we're in Logan's office to turn on a light. No point calling attention to us being here, if anyone happens to pass by."

Evie tried Logan's office door. "It's locked."

"Did you lock it when you left earlier today?"

"No, I'm sure I didn't. Someone else must have locked it."

"Do you have a key?"

"No, I only have a key to the side door and my storage room in the basement. Now what?"

Beth looked at the door in disgust. "I suppose we could try to pry it open or pick the lock. But I have no idea how to pick a lock. Do you?"

"No, I don't. And prying it open is not a great option. We'd probably lose our jobs if we broke in," Evie said.

"You're right." Beth yawned. "Okay. Whatever is in there will still be in there in the morning. Let's call it a night. I'm beat."

"Sounds good," Evie said. "Tomorrow I'll borrow the feather, so I can show it to you."

"Okay. I'm driving the bookmobile tomorrow morning. I'll be going past the Cedar farm. Maybe I'll stop in again."

"What for?"

"To talk to Ruth and try to find out what Bill asked her after he kicked us out. And I'd like to know if there were any large withdrawals from Vern's bank account, which might indicate that he was being blackmailed."

"You're relentless." Evie laughed.

*   *   *

The next morning Beth pulled into the driveway of the Cedar farm. There weren't any cars in the driveway, and nobody was around. She hesitated, then decided to see if anyone was home. Maybe Ruth had parked her car in one of the sheds.

She walked to the door, knocked, and waited. Nothing. She went into the porch and then tried the kitchen door. It was unlocked.

She leaned forward, hugging her shoulder bag to her side, stuck her head in, and called out, "Ruth, it's Beth. Beth Williams. Are you home?"

No answer. She tiptoed into the kitchen and called out again. Still no answer.

Beth stood there for a few moments, her heart beating loudly in her ears. Should she look around or come back later? She decided that, since she was already in the house, she might as well look around.

She made a quick circuit around the kitchen, opening and closing drawers, looking for a checkbook or any type of paperwork. But she found only the usual kitchen items.

She darted into the dimly-lit living room. The drapes were drawn, filtering the sunlight. It looked like an ad in a magazine. The furniture was a modern style, with bare wooden legs and arms and bright green and orange fabric cushions. The end tables were bare, except for large table lamps. A grouping of magazines was carefully fanned out on the coffee table.

A TV set and a record player sat atop a low wooden cabinet along one wall. It had three drawers in the middle, with sliding doors on each end. Beth strode over to it and quickly opened and closed drawers and doors. It held bottles of liquor, record albums, piles of magazines, and other odds and ends, but no paperwork.

They must keep their bills and mail somewhere, she thought.

She crossed over to a closed door, opened it, and found a staircase leading up to the second floor. Beth froze, her mouth dry and palms sweaty, wondering how she could explain what she was doing there if Ruth caught her in the house. *I might just have to resort to the truth*, she thought. There was no point trying to hide with the bookmobile sitting in the driveway.

Beth crept up the wooden stairs, pausing at every creak, listening for any sound indicating someone else was in the house. At the top of the stairs, there was a hallway with two doors in one direction and two in the other direction. She opened one of the doors on her right. It was a linen closet. She crossed the hall and opened the other door. *Ah-ha, a home office.* She went to the desk and opened the top drawer.

Yes! A checkbook. She opened to the register and glanced down the columns. At first glance, there didn't seem to be any unusual deposits or withdrawals. She didn't have time to examine it closely. She got her camera out of her bag, turned on the desk lamp, laid the checkbook open under it, and snapped pictures of the pages.

Once done, she replaced the checkbook and started rooting through the rest of the desk. The bottom drawer held file folders, labeled: taxes, bills, medical, and so on. She was rifling through them, and finding nothing out of the ordinary, when an envelope fell out of the one labeled "bills" and landed on the floor.

Beth picked it up and looked inside. With growing excitement, she saw it contained folded up notes. With shaking hands, she pulled out one of the notes and unfolded it. In large letters, it read "RETRIBUTION IS AT HAND." She mouthed, "Wow!" Here was the evidence she was seeking. It seemed someone really was blackmailing Vern.

Or were they? she asked herself. The note didn't demand money. But it was clear that someone was threatening him. If not money, then what did they mean to do, just frighten him? Or, had they followed through on their threats and killed him?

Beth refolded the note, stuck it back into the envelope, and put the envelope and her camera into her purse. Then she returned the folders to the bottom drawer, turned off the lamp, and left the room.

She started down the stairs, when she thought she heard something, froze in place, and listened. There it was again. It sounded like a groan.

She ran down a few steps but then stopped. *Maybe someone needs help?* she thought. She turned and crept back up the stairs, legs trembling, and paused at the top.

There it was again. The sound seemed to be coming from a room to her left.

She tiptoed to the door, slowly opened it, and peeked inside. Ruth was lying in bed, still in her pajamas, asleep. On the bedside table next to her was a half-full glass of water, an open bottle of pills, and a telephone.

"Ruth?" Beth said softly.

There was no response.

Beth went over to the bedside table and picked up the bottle. It was labeled diazepam. She wasn't sure what that was—probably some sort of sleeping pill. She set the bottle down. *How many had Ruth taken?* she wondered.

Beth reached down and jostled Ruth's shoulder, at first gently and then more vigorously. "Ruth! Ruth! Wake up!" she shouted as she shook her.

This elicited another groan, but Ruth didn't wake up.

Beth reached for the phone and dialed "O."

"Operator, give me the Davison City police," Beth said.

She heard a series of beeps. While being connected, she asked herself if she should be calling a doctor or an ambulance instead of the police. But the call went through before she could change her mind. She asked for Officer Crample, and he picked up right away.

"Bill, this is Beth." Her voice was shaking.

"Beth? What's the matter?"

"I'm out at Ruth Cedar's place. She's asleep and I can't wake her up."

"What? You're where?"

"I said, I'm out at the Cedar farm. Ruth is out cold. It looks like she took some pills, and I can't wake her up. What should I do? Should I call her doctor or an ambulance? I don't know the address. I—"

"Sit tight." He cut her off. "I'll send an ambulance. Got that?"

"Got it. Hurry!"

He clicked off. Beth put down the phone. She turned and stared down at Ruth. She was still breathing. There didn't seem to be anything else she could do for her.

Beth glanced around the bedroom. The bedspread, made of a frilly, pink material, was scrunched up at the foot of the bed. The closet door was ajar. It seemed packed full of her clothes. The top of the dressing table was covered with a jumble of jars of makeup, perfume, hairspray, hairbrushes, and the like. Where were Vern's things? Had Ruth already cleared everything out, or had he slept in another room?

Some of Ruth's clothes were piled on a chair in the corner next to Beth. A Dayton's shopping bag sat on the floor next to the chair. Beth peeked inside the bag. It was filled with new summer clothes, with the sales tags still attached. Maybe Ruth put it there when she returned from her weekend shopping trip and forgot about it after she found Vern's body. Beth picked up the bag and placed it on the foot of the bed.

Ruth groaned again. Beth paused and watched her sleep. She seemed to be breathing all right. Then, she turned back to the shopping bag, pulled the clothes out one by one, and piled them next to it. Then she pulled out a handwritten charge card receipt, listing all the clothing items, signed, and dated by a sales lady.

Beth couldn't help but notice that the prices seemed reasonable. A glance at the price tags showed they had been marked down. Beth smiled wryly at Ruth's apparent tendency to bargain shop for clothing, which contrasted with her expensive-looking living room furniture.

At any rate, it seemed that Ruth had an alibi. She really had been shopping on that Saturday, as she'd said.

Beth was removing the last few items when her fingers bumped against something solid on the bottom of the bag. She pulled it out. It was a box of Joy perfume, which was advertised as the most expensive perfume in the world. Beth turned the small box over, looked at the price tag, and whistled softly. This item cost more than the total of all the other items in the bag.

Puzzled, Beth took a second look at the sales slip. The perfume wasn't on it. So, how did Ruth buy it? Did she pay cash? No, if she had, there would still be a receipt. Had she put that receipt somewhere else? Or, did someone else pay for the perfume? If so, was someone else with her while she was shopping? Beth pulled out her camera and took a picture of the receipt.

Wailing sirens headed in their direction. Beth scooped the clothes and perfume back into the bag, put it back where she'd found it, and ran down the stairs.

Chapter 15

July 28, 1969

Ruth's doctor arrived around the same time as the ambulance. He assured Beth that Ruth would be all right. He said he had prescribed diazepam because Ruth was having trouble sleeping, but he hadn't given her too many, since it was—he hoped— a short-term problem. She may have taken too many, but it was unlikely to be serious. They would have to wait for the dosage to wear off. But he had Ruth taken to the hospital for observation, just in case.

Bill Crample arrived in his squad car shortly after the medical personnel got there. He paced up and down while they checked Ruth, loaded her into the ambulance, and left, and the doctor followed the ambulance.

Beth followed them out of the house. She saw Bill heading toward her, trying to intercept her, but didn't stop. "I have to go. I'm late for my route," she said as she passed him.

He turned and walked alongside her. When they got to the bookmobile, he placed a hand against the driver's door, preventing her from opening it. "This won't take long. What were you doing in the house?"

"I came to see Ruth. When she didn't answer the door, I tried it. It was open, so I went in."

"You came to see Ruth. Did she ask you to stop by, or was it your idea?"

She hesitated. *Darn, he saw through that answer,* she thought.

"She knew I was coming this way today. Maybe she wanted to chat with me about the questions you asked her last night after you kicked us out. By the way, why did you kick us out last night?"

He stared at her for a moment without answering, his eyes icy. "You know why."

"No, I don't."

"Didn't I tell you to keep quiet?"

"Yes, but—"

"Did you keep quiet?"

"No, but I asked a good question."

Bill sighed in exasperation. "Let's stick to what happened here today. Shall we?"

"Okay. As I said, I came to see Ruth. She didn't answer the door. I went in and found her unresponsive. It was a good thing I was here, wouldn't you say? Now, if you'll excuse me." Beth looked at her watch, then at his hand on the van door. "Or, do you intend to arrest me?"

He reluctantly removed his hand. "Not at the moment."

She squeezed past him and climbed into the driver's seat. Beth watched as he frowned down at the ground and felt a twinge of sympathy.

"Oh, by the way, I found something that you should have." Beth dug in her purse and handed him the envelope containing the threatening notes.

"What's this?" He opened it, pulled one out, read it, and then looked at her in astonishment. "Where did you get this?"

"I found it lying on the floor." She gestured toward the house.

"On the floor?" He sounded skeptical. "Where on the floor?"

"I don't recall exactly. I had nothing to do while I waited for the ambulance, so I did a little investigating. I looked around her room." That much was true, she thought, hoping he wouldn't notice that she'd changed the subject. "As you can see, someone was threatening Vern, maybe a blackmailer. Find that person, and you have your killer."

She started the motor. "I'm late. I have to get going."

"We'll need to talk to you more later," he said.

"Sure. I'll be home this evening. Call or stop by," she said.

Bill stepped back and raised a hand in farewell. Beth drove around the circular driveway and out onto the road with a sigh of relief.

Sunshine, Amber, and several kids were milling around the mailbox of Mellow Acres, waiting for Beth, when she pulled up a few minutes later. They all clambered on as soon as she opened the door and put out the step stool.

The kids all started talking at once and deposited piles of books on the small counter behind the driver's seat. When Amber and the kids moved to the shelves to pick out new books, Sunshine said, "We heard sirens. What was all the excitement?"

"That was an ambulance. That's why I'm late. Sorry about that," Beth said. "I stopped to see Ruth on my way here, and she was taken ill. I had to wait for help to come. They took her to the hospital."

"Hey, don't worry about it. Is she going to be okay?" Sunshine asked.

"Yes, I think so," Beth said. "But I'll have to cut my stop here short. I need to try to get back on schedule."

Unfortunately, little kids picking out picture books aren't easy to hurry, especially when their moms seem oblivious to the concept of hurrying.

Even if I skip lunch, I'll never make it to my next stop on time, Beth thought.

Miss Tanner had stayed late after the library closed to talk to Beth. Her red bouffant hairdo quivered, and her face was nearly as red as her dyed hair. She kept Beth standing in front of her at the circulation desk.

"I've been fielding calls from angry mothers all day, complaining that you were late. Maybe we need to find someone more reliable to drive the bookmobile. Where were you?"

Beth knew that word of what happened would soon reach Miss Tanner. Maybe she already knew about it. There was no point trying to cover up.

"I'm sorry. I fell behind. I tried to catch up."

Miss Tanner blinked. Apparently, she'd been expecting an argument, not an apology. She continued in a slightly less outraged tone. "What was it that caused you to fall behind?"

"I stopped in the see Mrs. Cedar, and it took longer than expected. She had some sort of medical problem. I had to call for help and wait for them to arrive," Beth said.

The color rose in Miss Tanners cheeks again. "You stopped for a visit while on the job?"

"I did. It was right on my way, and I didn't expect it to take long. I'm sorry if that was a mistake."

Miss Tanner lectured her on being responsible and sticking to the arranged schedule of stops. "We already added a stop, at your suggestion, to that other farm. See to it that you don't start adding all sorts of other stops along the way. It's not your personal vehicle, you know." She went on in that vein for a while longer and then asked, "What happened to Mrs. Cedar?"

"I'm not exactly sure," Beth said. "She might have taken too many sleeping pills. Her doctor came out, and an ambulance took her to the hospital."

"Oh, dear. That is shocking." She stared at Beth, one painted-on eyebrow cocked. "Does this have anything to do with your investigation into Vern Cedar's death?"

Beth looked at her with what she hoped was wounded innocence. "My what?"

"Come now, Miss Williams. Would you have me believe it's a coincidence that you just happened to stop by Ruth Cedar's farm, shortly after her husband is found dead in suspicious circumstances and your friend, Logan Rusk, is arrested?" Her eyes sparkled with curiosity.

Beth paused to think. Clearly, Miss Tanner was interested. She was well connected to the town's grapevine and might know something of interest.

"That's what I'd like to know. Why *is* Vern's death considered suspicious, and why is Logan a suspect? What have you heard?"

Miss Tanner quickly raised and lowered her eyebrows. "It's just gossip, really. It seems Mrs. Cedar may not have been completely satisfied with the life of a farmer's wife."

This statement surprised Beth. Usually, Miss Tanner was all business. Beth leaned forward. "I suppose that's so. She did seem interested in the theater. She tried out for a role in the play."

"But, was it the play or something else that she was interested in? Or should I say, someone else?" Miss Tanner said with a suggestive smile.

"I see," Beth said. "You're implying she was interested in Logan."

"He was a bachelor and nice-looking. I think that's all it took." Miss Tanner clamped her mouth shut. "But that's just gossip, as I said. Forget I said anything. Now, it's time we call it a day."

Chapter 16

July 28, 1969

Home at last. Beth exhaled in relief as she kicked off her shoes by the door. Chestnut followed her, meowing, into the bedroom while she changed out of her work clothes and into cutoff jeans and a sleeveless, striped t-shirt.

Then Beth padded barefoot into the kitchen, opened the fridge, and stared into it. There weren't many options. It was too hot to cook anything. It would have to be a bologna sandwich, chips, and bottle of beer for supper. She smiled, imagining what her mother would say about her meal choices.

Chestnut sat and looked at her, then up at the cupboard where Beth kept his food, and meowed again.

"Yes, all right. I haven't forgotten about you." She got out his food and poured some into his dish. "Happy now?"

It had been one heck of a day, between Ruth's overdose, the library patrons' annoyance with her because the bookmobile was late, capped off by being yelled at by her boss. Now, all she wanted was to relax and forget about everything for a while.

She carried her plate and beer into the living room, put it on the coffee table, opened a window to try to catch a breeze, and settled down in front of the TV. It had hardly warmed up when she heard a loud knock on her door. Oh, right. She'd told Bill he could come over. It looked like her day wasn't going to get any better. She reluctantly went to the door and opened it.

She was relieved to see Evie standing there. "Hey, it's you! Come on in."

"It's nice to be appreciated. Who were you expecting?"

"Bill Crample. And, in a bad mood."

"Why? What happened?"

"Come on in and I'll tell you all about it. I was just about to eat. Do you want something?" Beth gestured toward her food and beer.

"I'm not hungry, but I'll take a beer."

"Help yourself."

Beth returned to her spot on the couch. Evie got a beer out of the kitchen and then sat down on the other end of the couch. Chestnut settled, purring, between them.

Beth recounted what had happened, ending with, "So, I gave Bill the threatening notes that I found and said I'd talk to him later today. I thought he was at the door."

"Wow! What a day. You'd think Bill would be happy you found those notes and turned them over to him."

"You'd think. But, instead, he just got mad and wanted to know what I was doing in the house."

"What did you tell him?"

"I implied that Ruth had invited me, without saying so. I think he guessed I wasn't telling the whole truth, and he'll grill me for more details. I don't know what I'll tell him."

"The truth, I suppose. As long as . . ." Evie trailed off.

"As long as it doesn't make things worse for Logan," Beth said.

"Right. Hot, isn't it?" Evie took a sip of beer and lifted her long blonde hair off her neck. "So, did you recognize the handwriting on the notes?"

"I only looked at one note, but I think the handwriting looked the same as the note we found in Vern's coveralls."

"Probably. It'd be weird if he was getting threatening notes from several different people. Although, it's possible. He wasn't exactly Mr. Nice Guy."

"Yeah. We'll probably have a list of his enemies after we listen to the tapes of his shows. I'll go over to the radio station before work tomorrow and ask if we can borrow them."

"Speaking of borrowing things . . ." Evie started digging in her purse. "Ah, here's the feather I found in Logan's desk." She pulled out a red feather and handed it to Beth. "What do you think of this?"

Beth examined it. "It doesn't look natural."

"That's what I thought. It looks like it's been dyed, like a decorative one for a skirt, a vest, or a hat. Do you think it's like the one Vern had in his pocket when he died?"

"Could be. If so, that raises a lot of questions. Such as, why did both Logan and Vern have the same type of feathers? How did they get them? And why did they keep them? Was there a special significance to the feathers?"

A loud knock on the door interrupted Beth's train of thought. She gave the feather back to Evie, who stashed it in her purse.

This time, it *was* Bill, in uniform, at the door. She invited him in. He stood on her doormat looking bulky and out of place.

"Oh, hi, Evie," he said. "I didn't know Beth had company. I can come back later. Or you can come down to the station to make your statement," he said to Beth.

"That's okay. I was just leaving," Evie said and made a hasty exit. "See you later."

"Well, come on in and have a seat, Bill," Beth said. "Can I get you anything?"

"No thanks."

He took a seat in the chair across from Beth and put his hat down on the end table. Chestnut opened one eye, looked at him, then yawned and went back to sleep.

"Well, do you mind if I finish eating?" Beth asked.

"No, not at all." He fished a small notebook and a short pencil out of his shirt pocket. "I need to establish exactly what occurred at the Cedar farm. What time did you get there?"

"Let's see. I got to Plato around nine o'clock, stayed for two hours. Packed up and headed out. So maybe about eleven-fifteen or so."

"Was Mrs. Cedar expecting you?"

Beth took a bite of her sandwich and held up a finger, indicating "just a minute" while she slowly chewed and swallowed.

"Well, no. Not exactly."

Bill looked up from his notebook. "I thought you said she was expecting you."

"No, I said she *might* be expecting me, since that's the time I normally pass by."

"I see."

Bill stared at her for a long moment. Beth felt her face growing warm and took a sip of beer.

"And then you went into the house and started searching it. Is that correct?"

"Well, no. I knocked and called out. Then I went in and sort of started looking around."

"I see," Bill said and made a note. "And that's when you found Ruth?"

"Um, yes."

He consulted his notes. "Are you sure? I have a note here," he paged back in his notebook, "that you called the station at eleven-twenty-five. Are you saying it took you ten minutes to walk from your van to the house, enter, and find Ruth?"

"Well, I'm not exactly sure of the time."

Bill stared at her with his impassive cop face without speaking.

"Okay, so I looked around for a little while before I found her."

"While you were looking around, where exactly did you find the envelope of notes that you gave me?"

"Okay. If you must know, I found them in Vern's desk in his study. In my defense, if the police had done their job, they would have already found them."

He ignored her jibe. "And then you handled the envelope and the notes, destroying any fingerprints that there might be on the notes."

"No, that's not true. I did handle the envelope. But I only unfolded and read one of the notes, the one that read 'retribution is at hand.' You should be able to get prints off the others. Anyway, you have my prints on file from the last case that I helped you solve, so you can eliminate mine."

"Anything else that you can tell me?"

Beth thought about the bottle of perfume without a sales slip while she finished the last bite of her sandwich. She decided it wasn't worth mentioning. Maybe the sales slip had just been removed from the bag.

"Nope. I don't think so."

"Okay. I guess that's all for now." Bill flipped shut his notebook and stashed it and the pencil back in his shirt pocket. "I'll get back to you about any trespass or burglary charges."

"Burglary? What are you talking about?"

"You removed an item without permission. That's burglary."

"You mean the envelope?"

"Yes."

"Well, I gave it to you. So, I guess you're involved too. Maybe you should charge yourself. Anyway, I kind of doubt that Ruth would press charges after I saved her life," Beth said. "By the way, what did you ask her after Evie and I left last night?"

"I'm not going to answer that."

"Come on, I helped you out with a clue. It's your turn."

"You don't give up. Do you?" Bill seemed to be resisting the urge to smile. "Okay. I'll tell you this much, Ruth's alibi holds up. She gave me receipts for the hotel where she stayed."

"Thanks for that." Beth bit her bottom lip. Could she keep him talking? "One more thing, why is Vern's death considered suspicious? After all, it could have been an accident, couldn't it?"

"If the body had been badly mangled, we might have thought so. But the coveralls getting stuck prevented that. It appeared that he was killed by a blow to the head, which was unlikely to have happened accidentally."

Chapter 17

July 29, 1969

Beth called Don Winthrop at KROW first thing Tuesday morning and asked if she could stop by to learn more about Vern Cedar's radio show and listen to recordings of his show. He said that was fine.

When she got to the radio station, Don gave her a list of Vern's guests and the dates they had appeared. Then, he led her to the sound booth. A box containing reels of tapes sat on the desk next to a large tape recorder. He showed her how to wind the tapes onto the tape player.

"I'm sorry I didn't get back to you last week," Don said. "It got really busy here. I've been fielding calls from Vern's advertisers who want to cancel their contracts. None of our other shows have similar audiences."

"I understand," Beth said. "Did you get a chance to ask the station manager about angry or threatening calls from people that Vern bashed on his show?"

"I asked, and he said there were some complaints, but nothing that stood out," Don said.

"Okay. Well, thanks for asking." Beth sighed.

"Sorry I couldn't be more helpful," Don said. "Wait. I think there were some angry letters. I'll see if I can round those up. How long are you staying?"

"Until lunch. I have to work this afternoon. I don't suppose you have cassette recordings or eight-track tapes of the show that I could take home with me."

Don laughed. "Sorry, no. We're not that up-to-date. I'm afraid we only have these magnetic tapes."

"Okay. Well, thanks again. I appreciate your help. Is this all the tapes of his show?"

"Yes. He just started his show about six months ago. But his show was really catching on. He'll be missed."

Beth looked at the box full of tapes. "I won't have time to listen to all of them today. I guess I'll start with the more recent ones first."

Don showed her how all the knobs, buttons, and levers worked and then left her to it.

As Beth listened, she discerned a pattern. Vern ranted about various things, especially liberals, communists, hippies, and anti-war protestors, which he lumped together. He vented his ire on his guests or anyone who called to contradict or question him. Beth wondered why this repetitive format was appealing to so many people.

Her attention had started to wander when a call caught her attention.

"You don't know what you're talking about," a young man said.

"Is that right?" Vern asked.

"That's right. You're not going to be drafted and sent to some godforsaken rice paddy to be used for target practice."

"I served my country when I was called up. And you'd be proud to serve, too, if you weren't an un-American commie."

"You served? Where?"

"Where isn't important. The point is, I didn't dodge the draft."

The conversation continued until Vern finally admitted that he'd spent his time in the army as a driver in Germany.

"So, not exactly sitting in a foxhole, were you, Vernie?" the caller asked. Your biggest risk was getting in a car accident or maybe getting hemorrhoids from sitting on your ass—"

"That's all the time we have for our lefty-pinko caller, folks," Vern said as he abruptly ended the call and then went to commercials.

Beth chuckled to herself as she stopped the tape, beginning to understand how this kind of provocative programming could be fun. Then she paused. There was something familiar about the caller's voice. She rewound to the start of the call and listened again. What was it about that voice that was so familiar? Maybe Evie would recognize the voice. She knew most of the people in town.

There was a phone on the desk. Beth called the theater, got hold of Evie, and asked her if she could take a break and come over to the radio station. She agreed, and soon they were both in the sound booth listening to the recording of the call.

"What do you think?" Beth asked when it finished. "Do you know who he is? Does his voice sound familiar to you?"

Evie crinkled her forehead. "Nope. Sorry. But, play it again."

Beth rewound the tape and hit play and they listened again.

"Anything?" Beth asked.

"Wait. What's that sound in the background?" Evie asked.

"What sound?"

"Turn it up."

Beth turned up the volume, and they both concentrated on the background sound.

"Hear that?" Evie asked. "It's like a scraping or grinding of some sort."

"You're right." Beth turned up the volume some more and listened. "Oh, I know what that is!" she said. "That's the sound of someone grinding wheat. Now I recognize the voice. It's Lester."

"Who?" Evie asked.

Beth turned off the tape recorder. "One of the hippies, Sunshine's boyfriend, Lester. That's why he sounds familiar to me but not to you. You've never met him."

"Really? I thought they didn't have a phone."

"They don't now. I guess they did when Lester made the call. It must have been in their kitchen. At least, that's where Sunshine was grinding wheat while I was there."

"Are you going back out there to talk to him?"

"Not today, I have to work. Maybe tomorrow. Do you want to come with me?"

"Sure. I can take a couple hours off from work for that." Evie dug in her purse and pulled out a small manila envelope. "By the way, here are your photos that I developed."

"Oh, great. Thanks for doing that." Beth pulled them out of the envelope and started looking through them. "They're all pretty clear. I was worried I might have moved the camera or gotten too close and that they would come out blurry. But these look good."

"I noticed something. Take a look at that one of Vern's calendar," Evie said.

Beth looked at it. "What am I looking for?"

"Next to it, on the desk. See that pad?"

"Yeah. What about it?"

"Doesn't it look like the same size as the threatening note that Bill pulled out of the coverall pocket and showed us?"

Beth stared at the picture and then nodded. "Yeah, it could be. Well spotted."

"Of course, there are probably a million pads just like it."

"Probably. But it is an unusual shape—square, not rectangular." Beth stopped to think. "But why would Vern be writing threatening notes, and to who? It is very strange."

"We should check it out. You know how the detectives in fiction are always rubbing pads with pencils to see if there was an impression left from what was last written. We could try that."

"Okay. Let's check that tomorrow too."

Chapter 18

July 30, 1969

Beth had called to see if Ruth was up to a visit. After all, she had been taken to the hospital only a couple days ago. Ruth had sounded upbeat on the phone and invited Beth and Evie to come over.

Now, they sat at her kitchen table while Ruth bustled around the kitchen. She started a pot of coffee perking and then sat down.

"It won't take long," Ruth said, gesturing toward the percolator. She lit a cigarette and then held out the pack. "Want one?"

Beth and Evie declined, saying they didn't smoke.

"You seem to be in a good mood," Beth said.

"I am." Ruth smiled.

"Good," Beth said. "So, no lingering effects from the sleeping pills."

"Oh, no." She waved a hand dismissively, leaving a trail of smoke. "I forgot all about that after I got a call from Nigel Bergenson this morning."

"The director? What did he want?" Evie asked.

"He offered me the part of Lady Bracknell. I said yes, of course."

"Congratulations," Evie said. "It should be a lot of fun."

"Thank you. Of course, I'm a bit too young for the part. I would have preferred playing the role of one of the younger women, but I think I can make it work. I suppose they'll cast a high-school-aged girl as Gwendolen, so it won't be such a stretch to play her mother."

Evie glanced at Beth, who was suppressing a smile.

"I'm not sure. I'm just in charge of scenery," Evie said. "Nigel would be the one to talk to about casting,"

"Yes, of course. It's all so exciting. Isn't it? I'll have to be fitted for costumes, I suppose. Is Jessie Hanson doing the costumes?"

"Yes, that's right," Evie said.

"Of course, if we want the play to open on schedule, we have to get Logan out of jail," Beth said, trying to steer the conversation back to the reason for their visit.

"Oh, I know." Ruth's smile fell. "Are you any closer to proving his innocence?"

"No, not really," Beth said. "That's one reason we wanted to talk to you again, if you're feeling up to it."

"Of course. And, thank you for sending for medical help. Though, I'm now quite sure why you were here in the first place." Ruth's smile now looked forced.

"The same reason as now. I had some questions," Beth said. "I was driving past in the bookmobile and thought I'd just pop in. The door was open, so I stuck my head in when no one came to the door. I heard groaning, I went to investigate, and found you unresponsive."

"I see." Ruth looked at Beth through narrowed eyes. "Sure. Ask me whatever you want to. I don't have any secrets."

"Just to get the chronology straight, you drove to the cities on Friday afternoon, shopped on Saturday, and drove back on Sunday. Is that correct?" Beth asked.

"Yup, that's right."

"Is there anyone who can verify that? Did you meet up with someone while you were there?"

Ruth stubbed out her cigarette. "No. Why do you ask?"

"Just wondering," Beth said. "I thought maybe you met someone and went shopping together or something."

"No. I was on my own. I prefer to shop alone. No distractions while I hunt for bargains."

Beth thought about the perfume but decided not to ask about it now. She didn't want to admit that she'd been digging through Ruth's shopping bag while waiting for the ambulance to arrive.

"Okay. And you got home around what time?"

"I'd say around three o'clock. I stopped for lunch along the way."

"And, you found Vern's body in the grain bin several hours later. Is that correct? You said you wondered where he was, because he usually came in before that time."

Ruth closed her eyes briefly and then said in a low, husky voice, "Yes, that's right. Do we really have to go through all of this? The police have already asked me all of these questions."

"I'm sorry. I imagine it must be difficult," Evie said.

"I'm sorry too," Beth said. "I wouldn't bother you with all these questions, only the theater staff asked Evie and me to do what we could to try to clear Logan. Unfortunately, the police haven't shared everything with us. But we will understand if you don't feel able to—"

"No, no, that's okay. Go ahead," Ruth interrupted. "What else do you want to know?"

Beth pulled a small notebook and a pencil out of her purse and consulted her notes. "Sorry, just checking that I'm not forgetting anything. Oh yes. I wondered why you looked into the grain bin."

"What?"

"Was there any reason to think Vern might be in the grain bin?"

"I noticed that the access door was open. Vern had been loading grain and driving it to the elevator when I left on Friday. So, I thought he might be in there sweeping it out, getting ready for the next harvest."

"Wasn't that something that Dave normally did?"

"Usually, but sometimes Vern did it."

"That makes sense," Beth said. She consulted her notebook again. "And, when you found the body, was there anything about it that struck you as odd?"

Ruth went slightly pale. "Well, he was lying there, face down, and his pants were gone. The whole thing was beyond odd."

"And that's when you called the police."

"Yes, that's right."

"But not an ambulance."

Ruth grimaced. "No, not an ambulance. He was obviously dead."

Beth made a note. "On another subject, do you remember the threatening note that Officer Crample showed you?"

"Of course."

"Had you ever seen it before?"

"Um, no." Ruth got up abruptly. "Coffee, anyone?" she asked.

Beth and Evie accepted. Ruth unplugged the percolator, carried it to the table, and poured out cups for everyone, and then passed around cream and sugar.

Beth took an appreciative sip. "Anyway, to get back to what I was asking, you'd never seen that note, or any threatening notes, before. Is that correct?"

"I don't know. There might have been some. Vern had a way of antagonizing people."

"You mean, because of the show?"

"Well, yes, that. But there were other things too. He just seemed to rub people the wrong way. I think he liked stirring up trouble."

"In what way?" Evie asked.

"With the neighbors, for example. So what if a bunch of hippies moved in next door? The place was deserted and falling apart. It might as well be lived in. But Vern just couldn't stand them. He wouldn't shut up about it."

"That's very interesting. I went to the radio station and listened to some angry phone calls Vern got while he was on air. Did he get threatening phone calls at home?" Beth asked.

"Yeah, sometimes. But I can't tell you much about them. If a call was for him, and they seemed angry, I'd just hang up and then not answer the phone. I didn't want to get involved in any of that."

"I can understand that," Beth said. "One last thing, did Vern keep any records or notes about his show at home?"

"Not that I know of," Ruth said. "He may have kept something in his bedroom."

"You didn't share bedrooms?"

"No, he had his own bedroom. He snored. Anyway, the bedrooms in this house are so small that there was no room for all of our stuff in one room."

"Do you mind if we take a look at his room?" Beth asked.

"There's nothing there. I had Dave clean it out and get rid of his stuff. I couldn't face it."

"Okay, I think that's all the questions we have for now." Beth looked at Evie, who nodded in agreement. "Is it okay if we take a look around outside again? Evie might spot something that I missed."

"Sure, go ahead." Ruth lit another cigarette and waved them off. "I'll see you at rehearsals."

"Not exactly heartbroken, is she? It seems like she couldn't wait to get rid of any trace of Vern," Evie said as they walked to the shed where Vern kept his desk. "Not that I blame her."

"Me neither." Beth scanned the farmstead. "I don't see Dave around. I wonder what he did with Vern's stuff."

"Probably burned it, unless there was something he could use," Evie said.

When they got to Vern's desk, it looked undisturbed. Beth picked up the notepad, which was next to the calendar, and took a careful look. It was the sort of pad you might keep next to a phone to jot down messages. It was about five-by-five inches and gummed on one edge. She blew off a thin coating of dust, then sat down at the desk and rummaged through the top drawer to find a suitable pencil.

"Ah, ha. Here we go," Beth said, holding up a freshly sharpened pencil. "Now, let's see what we find."

She held the pencil sideways and rubbed the surface of the pad. A few shapes started to appear, but nothing she could make out. A few more shapes appeared. With growing excitement, she kept rubbing. But as the shapes appeared, she realized they were numbers, not letters. Certainly not large, angry letters like those in the threatening notes. Then, a plus sign appeared. With a sinking feeling, Beth realized this was math, not a message.

"It looks like arithmetic," Beth said as she handed the pad to Evie.

Evie held it up to the dusty window and tilted it back and forth, trying to get a better look. "Yeah, I think you're right. Too bad! So much for that clue."

"Not necessarily. Vern might have torn off a sheet before he wrote on it. The paper is about the right size and shape." Beth tore off the top sheet, folded it, and put it in her pocket. "I'm going to keep this and see if I can compare it to one of the threatening notes."

"So, that's the calendar in the picture." Evie flipped back a few pages, looking at Vern's notes. "More numbers. It looks like he was tracking prices."

"Yeah, that's what I thought too. Probably grain prices, trying to get the best price. With his wife's expensive tastes, I guess he had to."

Beth started digging through Vern's desk drawers.

"Hang on," Evie said. She picked up the calendar and held it up to the light. "Is this an R or a B?"

"What?"

"This note on July 4th. Look at it." Evie handed the calendar to Beth.

Beth took the calendar and tilted it back and forth. "You're right! I think it's a B 4:30. The bottom of the letter is written on a line, and it's faint. That's why I didn't see it before. So, Vern was meeting B at 4:30."

"Or something that he labeled 'B' was happening at 4:30. But it seems it didn't have anything to do with Ruth," Evie said.

"Help me look through his desk," Beth said. "Let's see if we can find a connection."

They dug through each drawer, filtering through old receipts, hordes of pens and pencils, old notebooks filled with numbers and dates, screwdrivers, keys, screws, nuts, and bolts.

Then, Evie held up a keychain with a small key attached. "Eureka!"

She handed it to Beth. The keychain was a small metal circle surrounding a cardboard center, labeled "B" in faded ink.

"Could this be it?" Beth wondered out loud. "It looks like a padlock key."

"Yes, it does." Evie took it back from Beth and examined it. "Do you think it has anything to do with the note? What do you suppose it opens?"

"Let's look around the farm and see if we can find a lock that it fits," Beth said.

They searched for over an hour but found nothing. They asked Dave when he came in from the fields, but he said he didn't recognize the key.

"Well, that's a dead end," Beth said, feeling worn out and discouraged. "Let's head down the road to the hippie farm and see what they have to say."

Chapter 19

July 30, 1969

"Here we are," Beth announced as she turned into the driveway of the hippie farm.

"Is it okay to just drop in?" Evie asked.

"I'm sure it's okay. Anyway, we kind of have to, since their phone is out of service. I see the phone line is still there." Beth pointed up to the line leading from the road to the house.

A couple of kids and several dogs surrounded their car as they parked and got out, only a few of the larger crowd of kids who had greeted her the last time she visited. Apparently, some of the visitors must have moved on.

"Hi, library lady," Jemma said as Beth got out of the car.

"Hi, Jemma. This is my friend Evie," Beth said. "Evie, this is Jemma. She's five years old, likes books and saying hi to visitors. Who's your friend, Jemma?"

"He's not my friend; he's my stupid little brother, Timmy."

Timmy stuck out his tongue at his sister.

"Hi, Timmy," Beth said. "Is your mommy around, Jemma?"

"Yup. She's in the house with Auntie Sunshine. Come on."

Jemma grabbed hold of Beth's hand and tugged her toward the house. Evie and Timmy followed.

They banged through the screen door and spilled into the house.

Jemma yelled, "Mom, the library lady is here."

Amber stuck her head out of the kitchen. "Oh, hi. Come on in. We're in the kitchen."

Beth and Evie followed her into the kitchen, and the kids trailed behind. Amber shooed the kids back outside to play and invited Beth and Evie to sit down.

Sunshine's baby boy, Silas, was crawling around on the floor. He crawled over to Beth and she picked him up.

"Uffdah, you're getting big," Beth said.

"Yes, and he's starting to get around and get into everything. Aren't you?" Sunshine smiled fondly at him.

Once everyone was introduced and settled, Sunshine resumed grinding wheat and Amber snapping the ends off of a big bowlful of green beans and dropping them into another bowl, leaving the ends on the table.

"I see your garden is still productive," Beth said.

"It sure is." Amber beamed. "I can barely keep up with it."

"Good thing it is," Sunshine said. "At least we have something to eat besides bread."

"You don't have any animals?" Evie asked.

"We have chickens. So, we get a few eggs, if we can find them before the dogs do." Amber laughed.

"No cows?" Evie asked.

"No, not yet," Sunshine said. "We have to buy milk for the kids. And, right now, we're all out," Sunshine said. She shot a worried look at Silas.

"Do you need to go to the store?" Beth asked. "I can drive you there."

"No, that's okay. We'll get by until the guys get back," Sunshine said.

"I thought it seemed pretty quiet around here. Where is everybody?" Beth asked.

"There's a music festival up by Devil's Lake. Everyone headed over there. Lester and Greg should be back soon. And, we don't know how many others they'll bring back with them. Hopefully, whoever it is, they'll bring something to share. But, they usually don't. I'm baking a lot of bread, just in case. So, at least we'll have bread and a big pot of veggie soup."

"Do you want some help doing that?" Evie asked Amber.

"Thanks, that'd be great." Amber shoved the bowls toward her.

"So, what brings you out here today?" Sunshine asked. "Is this about Vern's death?"

"Yeah, it is," Beth said. She looked around and spotted a black telephone on the wall, partially hidden by a pile of beat-up pots and pans. She pointed to it. "I see you have a phone. I gather it's out of service."

"Oh, yeah. It was here when we moved in. We had it connected and used it for a while. But it got too expensive," Sunshine said. "Why?"

"I just wondered. I thought you said you didn't have a phone."

"Well, not a working phone," Sunshine said.

"Sure, that makes sense," Beth said.

Silas was starting to fuss and squirm on Beth's lap.

"You can put him down," Sunshine said. "I'll keep an eye on him."

Beth looked at the surprisingly clean floor. She put the baby down, and he crawled under the table and disappeared.

"Also, I went down to the radio station and listened to some tapes of Vern's shows. I happened to hear Lester call into the show," Beth said. "You said you'd never listened to Vern's show, but I guess Lester did."

"Did he? I guess I forgot. Lester was always on the phone. That was one reason our bill was so high—Lester talking long-distance. I just wanted it for emergencies, but he was always yakking to someone," Sunshine said.

"In this case, he was talking about the draft," Beth said.

"Oh, yeah. I sort of remember that now," Sunshine said. "Lester is against the draft. Well, we all are. Why are we even involved in that war?" Sunshine stopped grinding and looked at Beth as though waiting for an answer.

"That's a good question. I really don't know," Beth said. "Do you, Evie? Evie's boyfriend is in Vietnam."

"He is? Man! That's a bummer," Amber said.

"Yes, I miss him," Evie said. "As for the reasons for the war, or if it's a good thing or a bad thing, I don't know. I just wish it was over."

There was a pause, while no one looked at anyone else.

Beth cleared her throat. "Anyway, as I was saying, Vern and Lester disagreed. Of course, that was Vern's stock-in-trade, arguing with callers. But I wondered if they might have argued about it in person."

"I don't know." Sunshine stopped grinding the wheat and glared at Beth. "But if you mean, do I think that Lester killed Vern, the answer is no. He wouldn't hurt a fly."

Sunshine's usual vague friendliness was gone. Now, she scowled at Beth, like a lioness protecting her cub.

Evie broke the tension by picking up little Silas who had pulled himself up and was clinging unsteadily to her pants leg. "Oh, what a big boy. I see you're learning to get around."

Sunshine smiled at them. "Yes, and getting into everything." She took a deep breath and started grinding the wheat again. "Anyway, Lester wouldn't kill anyone. That's why he doesn't want to be drafted."

Chapter 20

July 31, 1969

Beth didn't have to go to work until later, so she decided to do a little research. She went to the county clerk's office and filled out a request for plat books, one from the 1950s and a more recent one. Beth hauled the large, heavy books over to a table, opened one of the dusty books, and searched for the hippie farm.

She found the correct page and noted that in the 1950s the hippie farm had been the property of James Thornton. Wait. Wasn't Thornton Sunshine's last name? So, was James Thornton a relative? It was odd that she hadn't mentioned that.

Checking the more recent book, she saw that the Thorntons still owned just a little more than the eight acres that the homestead occupied. The rest of what had been Thornton land was owned by Vernon Cedar. Now, Ruth Cedar must own it, she supposed, and would probably put it up for sale as soon as she could.

That gives Sunshine a motive, Beth thought as she closed the books and returned them to the clerk. Except, where would

Sunshine get enough money to buy the land, even if it was for sale? Besides, Beth couldn't imagine Sunshine bludgeoning Vern and dragging his body into position to be mangled by the sweep auger. Although, she'd read that people could do amazing things when hyped up on adrenaline.

Maybe Sunshine had help. Was that the real reason that Lester and Greg were suddenly missing? She hadn't heard of a rock concert by Devil's Lake. But she hadn't been keeping an eye out for these things. Maybe the newspaper editor, Mr. Flack, would know.

She'd give him a call later from the library. He was usually a good source for all things newsworthy, and he owed her a favor after all the help she'd given him researching his book.

Beth's next stop was Mr. Nobis' office.

The secretary waved her through, saying, "Go on in. Fred is expecting you."

Fred? That's new, Beth thought. *Is his secretary hoping to be the next Mrs. Nobis, now that his wife left him? Luckily, he doesn't blame me for her leaving him. Although, he could, since she dumped him after some of his unsavory activities came to light during my first murder investigation.*

"Beth!" He smiled and stood up as she entered his wood-paneled office. "How's my favorite librarian slash private eye? Have a seat."

"I'm fine, Mr. Nobis. How are you?"

"I'm doing great, Beth. But please call me Fred. We're friends, right?"

"Sure. Okay, Fred."

As they sat down, Beth noticed he was wearing a jazzy new sport coat, rather than his usual dark suit and crisp white shirt. Apparently, he was trying to look more youthful, but the comb-over wasn't helping.

"To what do I owe the pleasure?" he asked.

"I want to update you on what I've found out so far."

Beth told him about her investigation.

"My, you have been busy. It sounds like Sunshine and her friends or the mysterious 'B' who Vern planned to meet, according to the note on his calendar, might be suspects. Thanks. Although it is far from proving Logan's innocence, I might be able to use some of that to muddy the water enough to cast doubt on Logan's guilt when he goes to trial."

"Has a date been set?"

"No, not yet. I'll let you know when I find out."

"I'd like to talk to Logan. Can I visit him?"

"I'm afraid that's out of the question. I'm the only one allowed to visit him. I can tell you that he's doing okay. Naturally, he's not happy. He maintains his innocence and is anxious to be released. I can act as a go-between, ask him your questions, and relay any information that seems appropriate and doesn't violate lawyer-client privilege. What do you want to know?"

"Well, besides how he's doing, I want to know if he was out at the Cedar farm on the weekend that Vern was killed. If so, why?" Beth explained how she'd overheard him admitting that he had been out to the Cedar farm. "And who might have seen him there?"

"Those are good questions." Fred made notes. "Have you asked anyone else that?"

"Yeah, Ruth and Dave, the hired hand, and the hippies. Ruth and Dave both said they were away that weekend, and the hippies said they didn't notice anyone or anything out of the ordinary, outside of the noise they heard on Friday evening."

"Hmm." Fred paused and drummed his fingers on the desk. "What do you make of the notes, the key, and the feathers?"

"I don't know. The notes have me really mystified. Why did Vern have that threatening note in his pocket when he died if the note came from the pad on his desk? Was he sending the notes to himself? That doesn't make sense."

"It is odd. Do you suppose someone else had a similar pad?"

"It could be, although they are an odd shape." Beth took the note she'd taken from the pad out of her purse and handed it to Fred.

"Why is this scribbled on?" he asked.

Beth smiled. "I was trying that trick you see in detective shows. You know, rubbing it with a pencil to see what was written on the previous note. But all we saw was numbers."

Fred held it up to his desk light and squinted at it. "Yeah, I see what you mean. What are these numbers?"

"Prices of grain, I suppose. It seems like he was waiting for the best price to sell."

"I don't know. These don't seem like dollar signs." He tilted up the lamp and held the note close to the light bulb. "Maybe this is 'oz.' I'm not sure. Do you mind if I hang on to this and see if I can get it enlarged?"

"Sure, that's fine," Beth said.

He looked at it again. "And it's a weird shape. Most notes are rectangular, but this one is square. But, if he bought the notepad locally, I suppose other people might have purchased similar items."

"True. I'll check the drugstore and the dime store and see if they sell anything similar. As for the key, it might be completely unrelated. I bet lots of people have old keys lying around that they no longer need. But, since it was labeled with a 'B' like the note on Vern's calendar, it might be relevant."

"And the feathers?"

"I have no idea. That's another question for Logan. Ask him about the red feather in his desk. Evie and I thought it was like the one that was in Vern's coverall pocket when he died. But we weren't sure, since Vern's feather was crushed. But they both appear to have been dyed red. We thought they might be from a piece of clothing, like a vest or a hat."

"Okay." Fred added to his notes. "I'll see what he says about that too. I'll call you after I talk to him. What's next for you?"

"Maybe a trip to the Twin Cities, if Evie is up for it. I'd like to double-check Ruth's alibi and see if anyone was with her on her shopping trip."

Beth explained about the perfume and the missing receipt.

"Have you asked Ruth if anyone was with her?"

"Yes. She said she was alone."

"I suppose Ruth could have just put that receipt in her purse, rather than in the shopping bag."

"True. It's a long shot, I know. At least we'll have an overnight shopping trip and eat at restaurants other than Big Boy or the Woolworths lunch counter."

"I suppose you must miss living in the city. How long has it been since you moved back home?"

"It's been about a year." Beth paused and thought for a moment. "Sure, I miss it sometimes. Mostly I miss the anonymity. You know, being an observer, rather than the observed."

Fred laughed ruefully. "Just wait, once you hit a certain age, you'll become invisible here too."

"No doubt. Anyway, I love spending time with family and old friends."

"And solving crimes?" Mr. Nobis winked at her with a dazzling smile.

Beth forced a small smile. *Is he hitting on me?* she wondered. *I hate it when someone winks at me.*

"Yeah, that too. It sure hasn't been dull. Well, I should get going," she said as she got up.

"Okay, talk soon," he said and turned off his smile.

With a sense of relief, Beth turned and left.

Chapter 21

July 31, 1969

Mr. Flack pushed through the library door, panting from the effort of climbing the outside stairs. Beth, who was seated at the circulation desk, raised a hand in greeting. He waved back and smiled as he waddled up to the desk.

"Sitting at work all day is not the best way to stay in shape," he said as he pulled out a handkerchief and wiped his brow. "It doesn't help that it is almost ninety degrees outside and humid."

Beth turned the oscillating fan, which had been pointed towards her, in his direction, and he leaned toward it.

"I know. Fortunately, it stays a few degrees cooler in here. With the fan going, it's almost bearable. I take it you got some information about the Devil's Lake music festival."

"Yes. I phoned a colleague at the *Daily Journal.* He said that there was supposed to be a music festival last weekend, but it got rained out. I'm sorry to say that if your young friends' husbands haven't returned home, they must have found other things to occupy their attention."

"That's not good." Beth thought about Amber and Sunshine and their kids and their lack of a phone, transportation, and groceries. "I suppose the guys decided to hang out with friends for a few days. Maybe they're already back with a reasonable explanation. Thanks for looking into that."

"No problem. After all, you were a big help while I was researching my book."

Beth suppressed a smile. It hadn't taken Mr. Flack long to turn the conversation to his favorite preoccupation—his book.

"How's that going?"

"Very well, thanks for asking. The University of Minnesota Press is going to publish it. I included you in the acknowledgements."

"Thank you. That was very kind. Be sure and let the library know when it is available. I'm sure Miss Tanner will want to include it in the collection. Have you settled on a title?"

"Yes, the title is *New Age Practices in Polk County, Minnesota*. I'll be sure to let you know when it's published. So, tell me, what's going on with the investigation? Have you made any progress?"

"Ah, so, I gather our investigation is common knowledge."

"Of course. You can't keep a secret around here. Logan's arrest created a sensation. Everyone says it couldn't possibly be him, and we're all rooting for you and Evie to crack the case. How's it going?"

Beth briefly outlined what they'd learned. "But I hope you're wrong about not being able to keep anything secret. It might be an advantage to keep certain facts secret until the right time, if you know what I mean."

"Absolutely. Mum's the word."

A young girl approached the circulation desk with an armload of picture books. Mr. Flack wandered off to browse through the newspapers while Beth checked them out, and then he returned.

"I was thinking that there was some controversy regarding the Thornton farm a while ago," he said.

"Really, what was it about?"

"Hmm. Was it something about poisons?" He pursed his lips. "No, it was pesticides, I think. Yes. That was it. That was shortly before the Thorntons sold out."

"Interesting," Beth said. "I think I'll swing by tomorrow. They might need a ride somewhere, unless the guys are back, and I might get a chance to ask about that."

"I hope it's fruitful."

"Say, do you know anything about the significance of feathers, especially red feathers?"

"Red feathers? Oh yes, you mentioned finding a couple of them, didn't you? Let me think. Well, red is usually associated with strength, courage, or passion. Of course, the Native Americans often used feathers in their rituals, dream catchers, headdresses, and so on. They may have included red feathers. I believe they especially valued eagle feathers. Of course, in other cultures, such as the native Hawaiians, red feathers were considered more valuable than gold."

Mr. Flack went on in this vein, while Beth waited for a chance to get him back on topic. At last, he paused.

"So, nothing specifically threatening or sinister about feathers that are dyed red?" she asked.

"Not generally, although it may have been intended as some sort of message. Most likely they were just dyed red for decorative purposes."

"Yeah, that's what I thought. Okay, well, thanks for the information."

Chapter 22

August 1-2, 1969

The next day, Beth called Evie.

"Can you take a couple days off from work?" Beth asked.

"Maybe. What do you have in mind?"

"First, check on how Sunshine, Amber, and their kids are doing. Then, a trip to the cities."

"Seriously? In our cars? That's a lot of driving for an overnight trip."

"I thought about that. How about if we go by train?"

After some discussion, Evie agreed.

Beth got a loaf of zucchini bread, which she'd made with her mom, out of the freezer compartment of her fridge to take with them to the hippie farm. She was starting to feel like she was overstepping her welcome and hoped the gift would gain her some goodwill. Then she headed out to pick up Evie.

They arrived at the hippie farm to find Amber and Sunshine sitting on the front porch on rickety wooden chairs, passing a joint back and forth while watching the kids play.

Jemma was carrying little Silas on one hip. Timmy raced around her, and then they all stopped, sat down, and looked at something that caught their interest. When they caught sight of Beth and Evie, they ran in their direction. This time, unburdened, Timmy was faster and got there first.

"Look," he said, holding out a white flower with a yellow center that he had plucked.

"Very nice. I think that's called a pearly everlasting," Beth said.

"Plasting," he said.

Beth smiled at his mispronunciation. "That's right, a pearly everlasting. Is that for your mom?"

"Uh-huh," he said. He turned and raced toward the house, holding the flower out in front of him. "Look, Mommy. I picked a plasting for you."

Beth and Evie followed him and joined Amber and Sunshine on the porch, who greeted them with slow, sleepy smiles.

"Hey, look who it is," Sunshine said. "What brings you back this way?"

"We thought we'd check in and see how it's going," Beth said, "and see if the guys are back or if you need anything for the kids."

"Groovy," Amber said as she examined the flower Timmy had given her. "This is beautiful." She ruffled his hair.

"I'll pick s'more," he said, turned, and raced away.

Jemma carried Silas up the stairs and put him down. "He's too heavy," she said, then ran off to join Timmy.

Silas crawled over to Sunshine, grabbed onto her long skirt, pulled himself up, and stood there unsteadily, smiling at his accomplishment.

"No, they're not back." Sunshine frowned. "They sent a letter saying they will be traveling with the band for a while. Now they're roadies."

"At least they sent us some bread," Amber said.

"Bread?" Evie asked.

"You know, moolah, money," Amber said.

"Oh, right. Well, that's good, I guess," Evie said.

"Speaking of bread, my mom and I made zucchini bread with some of your zucchinis, and I brought you a loaf," Beth said.

"Oh, wow! Thanks," Amber said, accepting it. "Would you like some tea? I was just about to make some."

Beth and Evie insisted they didn't want to be any bother, and Amber insisted it was no trouble. They eventually accepted the invitation, and Evie went into the house with Amber to help prepare the tea while Beth sat on the porch with Sunshine.

"So, it sounds like maybe Lester and Greg are going to be away for a while. How do you feel about that?" Beth asked.

"If they send money home, I guess it's okay," Sunshine said. "I just wish Lester had talked to me first."

"Yeah, I can imagine. Communication is a problem with couples," Beth said. "I know it was with me and my ex-boyfriend.

"Yeah? When was this?"

"We broke up about a year ago, and then I moved back home."

"Were you together for long?"

"Yeah, about ten years."

"Do you think you'll get back together?

"No, he married someone else."

"That's rough." Sunshine seemed to be thinking. "I came home too."

"You? What do you mean?" Beth tried to sound surprised.

Sunshine's face clouded over. "This farm is my home. Or, at least it used to be."

"Really? Why did you leave?"

"Vern and his dad drove my family away. I was just a little girl when we left. I don't think Vern even remembered me, but

I sure remembered him. He used to torment me when we were kids. He was a lot older than me and a bully, even back then."

Beth paused to think. "And that's what drove your family away? That a neighbor kid picked on you?"

"Not just that. Vern's dad was using a lot of pesticides. And, my brother was always getting sick. My mom thought the pesticides caused it. She convinced my dad to sell out and move away. My dad was never happy after we moved. He's a born farmer."

"I see. So, you blamed Vern and his dad for ruining things for your family."

"You could say that," Sunshine said. "So, forgive me if I don't feel too bad about his death, whether accidental or not."

"Does Lester know that?" Beth asked.

"Of course. That's why we could afford to live here without a regular income. Because it's rent-free. The Cedars bought our fields, but my family still owns the few acres that the farmstead sits on. And we're staying." Sunshine's eyes glinted with determination.

Soon Beth announced they had to be going, and they headed back to Davison City. Beth packed, arranged for her sixteen-year-old sister, Cathy, to feed Chestnut, and met Evie at the train depot.

As they drew near Minneapolis, Beth glimpsed the Foshay Tower. At thirty-two stories, it was the tallest downtown building. Throughout the years she'd lived there, it had been the first sight to greet her when returning from a visit home. During college and afterwards, while first dating Ernie, that sight had kindled a feeling of excitement. Later, when her relationship with Ernie soured, it had engendered a feeling of uneasiness. Now, she wasn't sure what she felt—mostly nostalgia for bygone days, she decided. They arrived at the Great Northern Depot, located on the northern edge of downtown, in the evening and got into a waiting taxi.

On the short drive to the downtown Radison Hotel, Beth soaked in the sights and sounds of the city that had once been so exciting to her. Evie, who had visited here occasionally for shopping trips or to go to shows, commented on the traffic and the number of people and stores.

They checked into their hotel room and quickly went out again for a late supper at the Nankin Restaurant.

"This is a welcome change from dinner at the Big Boy," Beth said, admiring the bright array of vegetables in the subgum she had ordered.

"I agree. So, what's the plan for tomorrow?" Evie asked as she scooped up a forkful of kung pao chicken.

"Go to Dayton's after breakfast and see if the salesclerk who helped Ruth is working. If she is, we'll ask her some questions. And, stop at the perfume counter and ask questions there too."

"Such as, was Ruth with someone," Evie said.

"Right. Then, do a little shopping, have some lunch, and then it'll be time to pack up and head home."

When Beth said "home" she meant Davison City, and it gave her a warm feeling. This city used to be her home. But that was when she'd hoped for a husband, children, and a home of her own. Now, it was just a place she used to live. Nice to visit, but not to stay.

"What's your theory? What do you hope to find out?" Evie asked.

"I don't have one yet." Beth impaled a broccoli spear with her fork. "Ruth has new clothes and a dated sales slip, which backs up her alibi that she was shopping in Dayton's on the weekend that Vern died. But she could have come back sooner than she said. So, I guess we could try to find out *when* she was shopping, if it was in the morning or the afternoon."

"It sounds like you think she did it."

"Well, it's often the spouse, at least in murder mysteries. What do you think?"

"I think Ruth is hiding something but not that she killed her husband. I don't see her as a killer. Maybe it's that she was seeing someone else."

"Yeah. I wonder about that too. I don't think she bought perfume for Vern's sake. She didn't even seem to like him very much at the end."

Evie blotted her sweating forehead with her napkin and gulped some water. "Wow! This stuff is hot."

"I warned you." Beth laughed.

"That's true. It's spicy but good, so I'm glad I ordered it."
Evie smiled and fanned her face with her napkin. "So, if Ruth
had a boyfriend, you think he might have killed Vern so he
could have Ruth for himself. Right?"

"It's a possibility," Beth said. "And, if we don't learn
anything new, at least we can do a little shopping."

They discussed various ideas of how to question the
salesclerks.

The next morning, Beth and Evie passed crowds of people
on the short walk to Dayton's. The tall brownstone building
occupied most of a city block. It was the largest of several
department stores near each other on the Nicollet Mall,
attracting crowds of shoppers.

During the work week, the crowd would have included
men in business wear. But now, on a Saturday, it was made
up mostly of women out shopping. Many of the women wore
dresses and heels. Some of the younger ones wore miniskirts;
others wore slacks. Some of the older women wore hats. Many
women toted shopping bags along with their purses.

Beth felt that she fit right in, wearing a dark blue pantsuit.
Her shoulder-length wavy hair was kept in place, to a degree,
with a wide headband that matched her outfit. Evie looked
spiffy in her red short-sleeved shift, with her long blonde hair
pulled back into a ponytail.

They passed through brass-handled double doors into
Dayton's. Inside, wide aisles and white walls and pillars gave the
store an open and airy aspect. The rumble of escalators provided
a background to the ringing of cash registers and phones and

the low hum of laughter and voices. They headed toward the escalators, passing the low glass cases which surrounded the pillars that displayed everything from cosmetics to scarves to perfume.

"Hey, let's look for the perfume that Ruth bought here," Evie said.

They circled several counters, staving off offers of spritzes of perfumes samples, until they got to the right one. Then, they waited while the salesclerk engaged in a lengthy conversation with an affluent-appearing woman, while they sampled several test bottles of various perfumes, sniffing each other's wrists.

After the salesclerk finished up her business with her customer, the phone rang, and she started what seemed like it might be a lengthy conversation with the caller.

"Let's go up to women's wear and circle back," Beth said.

"Sounds good," Evie said.

They rode the escalator several floors up to emerge into an expanse of various displays of women's workwear, sportswear, junior sizes, misses, and more. They browsed several areas that had clothing like those items Ruth had selected and, when a salesclerk approached, asked her if she knew Helen Moore, the name on Ruth's receipt. After several tries, they found someone who said they knew her.

"But she isn't here right now. She works in the afternoon," the salesclerk said.

"Only in the afternoon?" Beth asked. "Is that her usual schedule?"

"Yes, she never works in the morning, as far as I know," the salesclerk said. "And, we've both been here for several years. Is there something I can help you find?"

Beth declined, but Evie tried on and bought a couple new tops and then headed back.

"So much for that. I guess we'll never know what Helen Moore remembers about Ruth," Beth said as they rode the escalators down.

"No, but we do know that she was still here in the afternoon. That's something," Evie said.

"So, if she did drive home that day, it must have been in the evening or later," Beth said.

When they returned to the perfume counter, the salesclerk approached them, smiling. "Can I help you, ladies?"

"Yes, thank you. A friend of mine was here several weeks ago," Beth said. "Three weeks ago, to be exact. Would you have been working then?"

"I think so." The salesclerk looked puzzled. "Was there a problem?"

"No, not at all. She let me sample a perfume she bought, and I thought it was very nice. Although not exactly my style, I thought my mother might like it. Her birthday is coming up."

"What perfume was it?"

"Well, that's just the problem. I'm not sure. It was yellow. But that's probably no help. And it was in a large, rather square bottle, I think," Beth said.

"Oh, maybe you mean Joy." The salesclerk walked them down the counter and showed them a bottle.

"Yes, that might be it," Beth said. "What do you think, Evie? Is that the perfume that Ruth showed us?"

"It could be. Can I try some?" Evie asked.

"Of course." The salesclerk sprayed some on Evie's outstretched wrist.

Evie sniffed it and held it out to Beth. "What do you think? Is that the scent?"

Beth sniffed it and pulled a confused expression. "We've been trying so many scents, I'm just not sure anymore."

"That is a problem," the salesclerk said. "One can only sample so many scents at a time, and then the nose gets confused."

"Well, do you remember if this is what my friend bought?" Evie said. "She's a petite woman. Maybe she was with her husband."

The salesclerk leaned forward and dropped her voice to a confidential tone. "As a matter of fact, we don't sell too many of these larger bottles, because they are quite pricy. Let me think. Oh, yes. I think I do remember them. Is he an attractive, tall man with dark hair? Kind of artistic-looking, wearing a sort of flowered shirt?"

Evie glanced at Beth; her eyes widened in alarm.

"Yes, that sounds like him," Beth said, trying to sound casual. "By the way, how much does it cost?"

The salesclerk pulled a box out from the glass display case, turned the box over, and showed Beth the price sticker.

Beth raised her eyebrows and bit her lip. "Oh, I'm afraid that *is* a little too high for me. Sorry to waste your time."

"Not at all. Let me know if you see something else that you'd like to try." The salesclerk placed the box back in the display case and turned to help another customer.

"Did that description sound familiar?" Evie said as they walked back to the escalators.

"You thought it sounded like Logan, didn't you?" Beth asked.

"You thought so too. Didn't you?"

"I don't know. It was pretty generic—a tall, handsome man with dark hair."

"Yeah, you're right." Evie exhaled in relief. "It couldn't have been him. Could it?"

"Why don't you ask around at the theater? He was probably there that Saturday."

"I hope so."

"I bet he was. Meanwhile, let's put it out of our minds and do a little shopping," Beth said.

Beth bought a couple books and a large, slouchy leather purse with a shoulder strap and a fringe along the bottom.

"What are you going to do with that?" Evie asked.

"Carry stuff. The purse I have is too small. There's enough room in this bag for a paperback and all the other junk I haul around."

Evie laughed. "Eventually, that will be too small too."

Beth also bought a few baby outfits for her soon-to-arrive niece or nephew. Then, they had lunch at the Dayton's Sky Room, including an order of their famous popovers, before heading back to the hotel to pack and then home.

Chapter 23

August 3, 1969

Beth sat with her family in her parents' living room, sipping coffee after the big midday Sunday dinner, and smiled as she watched her very pregnant sister-in-law, Debbie, pull tiny terrycloth sleepers out of the small Dayton's shopping bag and hold them up for everyone to admire.

Beth's mother, sister, and Debbie oohed and aahed over each one, the green one with an embroidered baby duck holding an umbrella on it, the little yellow one with an embroidered teddy bear on it, and the red-and-white polka dot one with an owl appliquéd on it.

"You shouldn't have," Debbie said. "You already gave us such nice shower gifts."

"I couldn't resist. They are so cute," Beth said. "I can't wait for him, or her, to be born. Then I can buy blue or pink things too."

"You're carrying it high—a sure sign that it's a boy," Mom said.

Beth's mom and Debbie then launched into lengthy speculation about the likelihood of a boy or a girl.

Beth's brother, Gary, the father-to-be, and Beth's dad watched with affectionate disinterest and then went back to discussing whether the Twins would beat the Orioles in today's game. Soon, they ducked outside to sit in lawn chairs under a shade tree and listen to the ball game on the radio.

Mom turned to Beth and asked, "So, you and Evie went to the cities. What did you do there?"

"Not much. We went to a Chinese restaurant for dinner on Friday night, shopped yesterday morning, and then came back home yesterday afternoon. It was a quick trip."

"Chestnut missed you," Cathy said. "When I went to feed him yesterday morning, he was very clingy, so I stayed and played with him for a while."

"Thanks for taking care of him. He seemed happy to see me when I got home," Beth said. "Although, I think he just likes his routine and knowing there is someone there who will feed him."

"Did you go just to shop?" Debbie asked.

"Yeah, pretty much," Beth said.

Her mom looked at her skeptically. "I bet there was more to it than that. I hear you are looking into what happened to Vern Cedar."

"Who's that?" Debbie asked. "I've been pretty much out of the loop, focusing mostly on getting ready for the baby."

"You know, the radio talk show host who died," Mom said.

"Oh, him," Debbie said with a look of disgust. "I never cared for that show. I turned off the radio whenever it came on. But why is Beth looking into what happened to him?"

"Well . . ." Mom said. Then she stopped abruptly and turned to Cathy, who was listening with rapt attention. "Cathy, don't you have homework to do?"

"Oh, Mom! I have plenty of time to do it later."

"You'll do it now. Or there'll be no television after supper."

"Okay, okay. But I'm going to find out what you're talking about later anyway. I'm not a child," Cathy said.

They watched as Cathy stomped out of the room.

"As I was saying," Mom said in a confidential tone that caused Beth and Debbie to lean in, "the police think Vern was murdered, and they arrested Logan Rusk."

"That nice theater teacher?" Debbie said. "When did this happen?"

"Last month," Mom said, looking at Beth, who nodded in confirmation.

"That can't be right," Debbie said. "I know Mr. Rusk. He was a teacher when I was in high school. He wouldn't hurt a fly."

Beth was a little taken aback by hearing Logan referred to as "Mr. Rusk" and the realization that Debbie, who was twenty-two, had been in high school only a few years ago. The eight-year gap in their ages suddenly seemed a chasm.

"That's pretty much what everyone thinks," Beth said.

Debbie paused. "So, you and Evie are looking into it, since you helped solve a couple of other cases. Is that it?"

"That's part of it. Logan is trying to open a theater here in Davison City. You know about that, right?"

Debbie and Mom nodded.

"Evie took the job of stage manager, and I help her out. Anyway, the rest of the theater crew asked us to discover the truth about what really happened. They can't go on for long without Logan. So, we said we'd try to find out."

"And, have you figured it out?" Debbie asked.

"Not yet. We have some bits and pieces, but they aren't fitting together," Beth said.

"I still think it was just an accident," Mom said. "Farming is dangerous. Everyone knows someone who was hurt or killed in a farming accident. For example, my Uncle Frank lost several fingers trying to unclog a cultivator." She went on to describe several other grizzly accidents.

"I suppose it could be an accident," Debbie said. "But the police must think it was murder. Do you know why? Or why they thought it was Logan?"

"I really don't know, and I'd better not say too much. It's just speculation at this point," Beth said.

Beth sipped her coffee and pondered how much she should say. If Debbie repeated something Beth said to Gary, and he then mentioned it in his auto repair shop, it would be all over town in no time. As for Mom, one trip to the hairdressers or a meeting with her craft circle, and all her secrets would be spilled. On the other hand, maybe they could help her fill in some blanks. It might be worth a try.

"There is one thing . . ." Beth hesitated.

"What?" Debbie and Mom said in unison and leaned toward her.

"It seems like someone claimed to have seen Logan out at the Cedars' farm on the weekend that Vern was killed. But I don't know if he really was out there. If he was, I'd like to know who saw him."

They leaned back and seemed to be mulling it over.

"He went there to see Ruth, I suppose," Mom said.

"Possibly," Beth said. "It depends on *when* he was out there. If he was out there on a Saturday afternoon, he couldn't have seen Ruth. She was in Minneapolis, shopping in Dayton's, that Saturday afternoon. We know that much. But she may have left home later on Friday or come home earlier on Sunday than she claimed."

"I get it," Debbie said. "That's why you went to Dayton's, to check up on Ruth's alibi."

"Well, we hoped it would work out that way," Beth said. "And it kind of did."

Debbie turned to Mom. "Why do you think Logan went to see Ruth?"

"Because she's, I really shouldn't say, but she's kind of wild. Anyway, that's what I hear," Mom said. "That she's kind of a man chaser."

Beth thought of the perfume salesclerk's description of the man who was with Ruth. It could have been Logan, although she hated to think so. On the other hand, if he was with Ruth, they both had an alibi. *Or they killed Vern together*, a niggling voice at the back of her mind added.

"I suppose Vern and Ruth might have met up and gone to Minneapolis together," Beth said. "But would he pick her up right under Vern's nose? I doubt it. More likely, she would drive to his house."

"If they drove out of town together, someone was sure to have seen them. And maybe they mentioned it to someone else. Leave it to me. I think I'm due for a trip to the salon," Mom said. "More coffee or another piece of pie, anyone?"

Beth and Debbie both declined, saying they couldn't eat or drink another thing.

"Then, you each have to take some pie home with you," Mom said.

When Beth got back to her apartment with a Tupperware container with several pieces of pie in it, she called Evie to let her know that her mom and sister-in-law were on the job, tracing Logan's movements on the weekend of Vern's death.

"Are you sure that's wise? That will pretty much let everyone, including the murderer, know that you're on the case."

"No. I'm not sure it's wise. But I think that our investigation is an open secret already."

"Yeah, I suppose you're right about that. After all, the theater staff asked us to investigate, so they know, and our families, and Bill Crample, and the people we've questioned. It's kind of out there."

"Not to speak of the radio station, my boss, Logan's lawyer, and others. I guess if we wanted to keep it secret, we did a crappy job."

Evie laughed at that. "Speaking of jobs, can you help me work on props this week? I'm kind of behind after taking a couple days off to go to the cities."

"Sure. I'd be happy to."

They discussed their work schedules and agreed to meet at the theater on Tuesday morning.

Chapter 24

August 4, 1969

Beth parked the bookmobile next to the hippies' mailbox, opened the sliding door, put out the step stool, and honked the horn. A few minutes later, she heard a screen door slam. Sunshine approached, carrying Silas on one hip and a bag full of books in her other hand. Beth hopped down from the van, hurried to meet her, and took the bag of books from her.

"On your own today? Where's Amber?"

"She got a letter from Greg and decided to join him. He's somewhere in New York with Lester and the band."

"New York City?"

"No, some town in rural New York. Woodstock, I think she said. I guess there's going to be a big music festival out there in a couple of weeks, and they're going to hang out until that happens."

They arrived back at the bookmobile. Sunshine put Silas down inside. He started crawling around, and she sank down onto the reading bench.

"Is Lester staying out there too?"

Beth deposited the books into the return bin, gave the bag back to Sunshine, and sat down in the driver's seat.

"Yeah, it's just me and Silas for the time being. Maybe that's not worth the extra drive for you."

"Oh, I don't mind. It's just a few minutes from Plato to here. But, are you going to be okay on your own? It must be a big change, from a houseful of people to just you and the baby."

"It *is* kind of spooky at night. But it won't be for long. My parents are coming out for a couple weeks to help out. You know, to get the house in order. The roof needs to be patched. Rain pours into one of the bedrooms every time it rains. And I want to get the electricity and phone switched on."

"That sounds good."

"Yeah, it will be nice. Except I'll have to stop smoking weed while they're here." Sunshine laughed. "But, that's okay. We're nearly out anyway. So, no extras for my friends or yours."

"My friends? Which friends?"

"Oh, that's right. He's not around anyway."

"You've lost me. Who's not around?"

"Your friend, Logan. Is he still in jail?" Sunshine pointed to the theater poster. "What's happening with the show?"

Beth's mind raced. "You mean . . . Logan was out here?"

"Oh, yeah." Sunshine scrunched up her face. "I forgot. He said we shouldn't tell anyone. Don't repeat that."

"Don't worry about it. Logan is in a lot bigger trouble than just getting busted for, what, buying dope?"

"Yeah. Normally, we would have just given it to him. But he offered to pay, and we kind of needed the bread. You know."

"Sure. That makes sense," Beth said. "When was that?"

Sunshine jumped up and retrieved Silas, who was pulling picture books off the bottom shelf, sat back down, and jiggled him on her knee.

"Let me think . . ." Sunshine stared off into space. "Just before Vern died, I think. Yeah. The day before all the cop cars were racing around and everything."

"No kidding? Did the police ask you about that?"

"Not me. I never talked to the police. Nobody did, as far as I know. If they had, I'm sure I would have heard about it. You're the only one who ever asked us anything about it."

Beth half-listened as Sunshine chattered on, while she tried to work out the significance of this new information. Why hadn't Logan told the police that he was out this way to see the hippies, not to see Vern or Ruth? Was he worried about getting in trouble for buying weed or worried about getting the hippies in trouble for selling it? Surely being charged with murder was much more important than that. Or, was it something else? Had he also stopped next door at the Cedar farm that same day? When Beth tuned back in, Sunshine was talking about Lester.

"The thing is, Lester is all about roughing it, living off the grid and all that. But, he's not here, and I have the baby to think about."

"Sure." Beth nodded in agreement. "Will he be mad when he gets back?"

"Maybe." Sunshine laughed. "But he'll adapt. Anyway, I'll put the utilities in my name, so he can still be off the grid."

"I guess you don't have the same last names. I take it you two aren't married."

"Nope. He says marriage is bourgeois. I think he just wants to keep his options open."

Beth was tempted to say that Sunshine could do better. But then she looked at Silas, who no doubt needed his daddy, and decided to keep her opinion to herself.

"Maybe he'll come around. What do your folks think about all that?"

Sunshine laughed. "Well, they're not too thrilled, especially my dad. So, the timing of their visit is good. I won't have to listen to my dad fighting with Lester."

Beth helped Sunshine pick out some books and then hit the road. She was eager to finish work and discuss this information with Evie.

Later, Beth and Evie shared a corner booth at the Pig and Whistle, where they could keep an eye on who was coming and going. They discussed the latest developments over burgers, fries, and beers.

"Sunshine said what?" Evie asked, leaning in.

"That Logan was out at their place on the weekend that Vern died." Beth glanced around to be sure they weren't overheard. "He went out there to buy some weed, which explains why Logan was out there."

Evie sat back and stared, open-mouthed. "I can see why he wouldn't want to admit that. His job would be on the line, and the hippies would be in trouble for selling weed."

"Maybe. But who do you think ratted him out to the cops?"

Evie thought for a moment while she salted her fries. "Well, it certainly wasn't the hippies or Logan. So, who does that leave?"

"It could have been Vern," Beth said.

"What?" Evie exclaimed.

"Sure. He could have called the cops before he was killed. He wouldn't have had any way of knowing for sure what Logan was doing at the hippie farm, but he might have guessed and made an anonymous complaint just for spite. Vern was fond of stirring up trouble."

"That makes sense." Evie put down her burger, wiped a small blob of mustard off her lip, and stared at Beth, her forehead wrinkled in worry. "Wait a minute. If Vern turned Logan in for buying weed from the hippies, that means . . ." She looked at Beth in alarm.

"Yeah, I'm afraid it might look like a motive for killing Vern," Beth said. "I've been worrying about that all day,"

"He didn't do it," Evie said. "I'm sure he didn't."

"I don't believe he did it either. Unless it was an accident, if they got into a scuffle, and Vern fell and hit his head or something," Beth said. "We need to know when these things happened. When did the police get the tip about Logan, and when did Vern die? If we knew that, then that would tell us a lot."

"Right. If the police got the tip about Logan after Vern died, then it had nothing to do with Vern's murder. Do you think Bill might tell us that?"

"Maybe, if he knows. We can ask." Beth took a bite out of her burger.

Evie pushed the fries around on her plate. "Logan admitted that he'd been out that way. Didn't he?"

"Yes. He said something like, 'So I was seen out there. So what?' When I overheard him talking to some woman at the theater."

"Did you ever find out who she was?"

"No. They were on the other side of the stage curtain. And I never got a chance to ask him."

"It must have been Jessie. She's the only woman on staff besides the two of us," Evie said. "She'll be there doing some costume fittings tomorrow. I'll ask her."

When Beth got home, she called her mom and asked if she'd heard anything about Logan's whereabouts on the weekend that Vern was killed.

"According to the grapevine, his next-door neighbor said he thinks that Logan was away from home most of the day before Vern's body was found. Of course that doesn't mean much. Maybe he was at the theater."

"Or the neighbor was mistaken," Beth said.

"That could be too," Mom said.

Beth hung up the phone with a heavy heart. Things didn't look good for Logan.

Chapter 25

August 5, 1969

Beth dipped a paintbrush into a small cup of black paint and carefully outlined fake bricks onto the fireplace mantel. It was part of the morning room décor in the opening scene of the play. Although constructed of balsa wood, cardboard, and canvas, the fireplace looked convincingly real. She stepped back and admired her work.

Evie stood at the worktable, glueing together an assortment of sticks that would fit inside of the fireplace when it was done. She turned to look at Beth's work.

"That looks great. You've really gotten the hang of it."

"Thanks, I thought so," Beth said.

Evie glued the final stick to the top of the woodpile. "What do you think?"

"Perfect," Beth said. "Are you ready for a break?"

"Sure. Shall we?" Evie pointed to the side table with a coffee pot and box of doughnuts on it.

"Sounds good. But first I want to call Mr. Nobis and see if he has any news. I'll use the phone in Logan's office."

A few minutes later, Beth was on the phone with Mr. Nobis.

"Did you get a chance to talk to Logan?" she asked.

"Yes, I did. I'm sorry I didn't get back to you. My secretary tried to call, but you must have been out. Are you at home now?"

"No, I'm calling from Logan's office at the theater. Sorry I missed your calls."

"That's okay. Clearly, you are a busy lady."

"So, what did Logan say? Did he admit being out at the Cedar farm on the weekend that Vern was killed?"

"He said he was not at the Cedar farm. But he may have been in the area. I'd rather not say any more than that."

"You don't have to. I found out Logan went out to the hippie farm that weekend to buy weed. Did Logan know who saw him?"

"No, he didn't." There was a pause. "I assume one of the hippies told you about Logan's visit. I'm sure you can appreciate that it's best not to spread that information around. Who else knows?"

"Let's see. Evie knows, for one. And, as I mentioned before, I think our wardrobe lady, Jessie, knows. She might have told other people. But she never mentioned it to me or Evie, so it seems she's keeping it to herself."

"That's good. The less said about it, the better. As you may know, possession of marijuana, even a small amount, is a felony under the Boggs Act."

"But Jessie might be able to tell us who saw Logan out there that weekend. And that person might be another suspect, or they might have seen something that would help clear Logan."

"I get it. But let's hold that in reserve for now. If anyone needs to talk to Jessie, I'll do it, if that's our only option. It doesn't make sense to clear Logan of murder, only to cost him his job or, God forbid, send him to prison for possession of a controlled substance."

"I see your point. Okay, I won't mention it. What about the feather? What did Logan say about that?"

"He seemed genuinely mystified. He didn't recall picking up a red feather or seeing one in his desk. Maybe it's unrelated."

"Or, maybe someone else put it in his desk."

"I suppose that's possible. In other news, I enlarged the note that you gave me."

"Really? What was on it?"

"I think I'd rather show you. Are you working at the library tonight?"

"Yes."

"Good. I'll see you soon."

Beth decided to take a closer look at the feather. She dug around in Logan's desk and pulled it out. It was large, possibly from a goose or a heron. She ran it through her fingers. Flakes of red paint came off on her fingers. Under the paint, it appeared to be gray with white at the base. She took it backstage with her. Beth told Evie what Mr. Nobis had said.

"Okay," Evie said. "If that's what he thinks is best for Logan. I guess we won't ask Jessie about it. Good thing you talked to Mr. Nobis first."

"I guess so," Beth said. "Oh, and while I was in Logan's office, I decided to take another look at this." She dropped the feather on the table, got some coffee and a doughnut, and sat down. "Look at it. The paint is flaking off."

Evie picked it up. "I'll say. It looks more like a water-based paint than a dye. If it was dyed for decorative purposes, they sure did a lousy job." She took the feather over to the sink and let the water run over it. "It's rinsing right off."

She blotted it with paper towels, returned to the table, and laid it down between them.

Beth picked it up. "It almost looks like an eagle feather. But it can't be."

"Why not?"

"Well, for one thing, there are hardly any eagles left. They're on the endangered species list. They've been hunted and poisoned by DDT to near extinction," Beth said. "I've helped kids do term papers on eagles; that's why I know about that. It's probably just a turkey or goose feather."

"Whatever kind of feather it is, why was it painted red? And why was it in Logan's desk?" Evie asked.

"I don't know. I could bring it to the library with me this afternoon, do some research, and try to figure out what kind of bird feather it is."

"That's a good idea," Evie said. "And you could show it to Mr. Nobis when he stops in."

The library was quiet that evening. In the summer, kids didn't have homework, and most people liked to spend the long evening hours, when daylight lingered, outside or in front of their TVs. Only an occasional visitor stopped by to read the newspapers or return a book.

Beth enjoyed the absence of interruptions. She reshelved books and then inserted title, author, and subject cards—for the library's newly acquired books—into the card catalog. Then, she pulled some bird identification books from the nonfiction shelves and took them to the circulation desk with her. She browsed through several until she found one with pictures and descriptions of feathers. After comparing her feather to several other species, she turned to the section on eagles and compared her feather's size, shape, and coloring. It seemed to match.

She looked up when the front door opened. Mr. Nobis strode in, looking like a car salesman in a madras jacket that highlighted his fake-looking tan face, which set off his gleaming white teeth. From his casual dress, it was obvious that he had not been in court today.

"Hello, Mr. Nobis."

"It's Frank, remember?"

"Right. Hello, Frank. So, what is it that you wanted to show me?"

He glanced around and noticed an elderly man, who had been perusing the newspapers, looking in their direction. "Is there somewhere private we can talk?

"How about in Miss Tanner's office?" Beth placed the "ring bell for service" sign next to the bell and started toward the office.

Mr. Nobis followed her around the circulation desk. "Hang on." He stepped over to where Beth had been sitting and picked up the feather. "Is this the feather you mentioned?"

"Yes, that's it."

"But it's not red."

Beth explained how they had rinsed off the red paint. "I think it might be an eagle feather."

"I see." His tone was neutral. "Lead the way." He gestured with the feather.

Once they were in Miss Tanner's office, he turned toward her and pointed the feather in her direction. "It's illegal to have these, you know."

"Illegal? Why would it be illegal?"

"Because of the Bald Eagle Protection Act. And, why would you rinse off the red paint? You must realize that it's not a good idea to tamper with evidence."

Beth felt like she was being cross-examined. She felt her face getting hot.

"How could it be tampering with evidence? It's just a feather we found in Logan's desk. It may have nothing to do with the case."

"Clearly, you thought it was related to the case, though. Didn't you? Otherwise, you wouldn't be so interested in it."

Beth stepped behind Miss Tanner's desk. She wanted to give herself a moment to think and to put an obstacle between her and her interrogator.

"I thought it might be related. It's kind of like the feather that was in Vern's coverall pocket. Although, that one was crushed."

"Where is that one?"

"The crushed one? The police have it."

"I see." Suddenly Mr. Nobis' demeanor changed back to relaxed friendliness. "Well, don't worry about it. You didn't know. Tell you what, I'll hang on to this for the time being and see that it gets into the right hands after Logan is cleared."

Beth nodded. "Okay."

She was a little unsettled by the quick changes in his demeanor, from friendly to accusatory and then back to friendly. She was glad he was on her side. At least, she hoped he was.

"You were going to tell me about the note," she said.

"Oh, yes." He pulled an envelope out of his inner jacket pocket. "I had it enlarged."

He unfolded a legal-sized sheet of paper and handed it across the desk to her.

Beth switched on the desk lamp and placed the document under it. It was blurry and streaked, but it seemed to be a list of weights and prices. The weights were in ounces. The corresponding prices were in the hundreds of dollars.

"That's a lot of money for not much," she said. "What do you suppose it means?"

Mr. Nobis shrugged. "I can't say for sure. If I guessed, I'd say it's drug prices."

"Drugs?" Beth stared at the numbers. "I suppose that could explain it."

"Explain what?"

"Where the money came from. Ruth has expensive tastes." Beth told him about Ruth's new furniture, clothes, and perfume. "I figured she was running up debt, and that's why Vern was so intent on getting the best price for his crop and why he took the radio talk show job. But maybe it went farther than that. Maybe he was dealing drugs. Maybe they were both in on it."

"That's a lot of maybes," he said. "I suppose if Vern was dealing drugs, that would give someone else a motive—a drug deal gone bad, that sort of thing." Mr. Nobis tapped his fingers on the edge of the desk. "But we don't have any proof."

Beth thought of the key and the mysterious "B" on Vern's calendar. But she decided not to bring it up. She wanted a chance to talk it through with Evie and decide what to do next.

"Do you mind if I keep this?" She indicated the enlargement.

"No, that's fine. I have other copies."

"Okay, well, thanks for stopping by." She switched off the desk lamp. "I'd better get back out to the circulation desk now."

Chapter 26

August 6, 1969

Beth rolled over in bed, dislodging Chestnut, who was purring on top of her. Through closed eyes she saw flickering shadows of the morning light that poured around the edges of her bedroom curtains. She yawned, stretched, and then sat up. She was in no hurry to start the day. All too soon, summer would be over, and the pace of life would accelerate. She would have to wake up to an alarm and then rush off to work or school.

Then she remembered that she had a mystery to solve, and her eyes flew open. Almost three weeks had passed since Logan was arrested. She imagined him behind bars, waiting and hoping that today might be the day he would be released. She needed to expose the real killer and get Logan released. But how? She had too many questions and not enough answers.

She pondered her next steps as she got dressed, fed Chestnut, and then sat down with her breakfast. Then the phone rang. It was her dad.

"Hi, sweetie."

"Hi, Dad."

"I hope I didn't wake you."

"No, I've been up for a while. I'm just having breakfast. What's up?"

"Well, I know you have the day off, and I was hoping you might be able to go with me on a job."

Beth's heart sank at the thought of spending the day holding a ladder or handing him tools. "Um, maybe. I told Evie I would check in. She might need help at the theater. What kind of a job?"

"Don't sound so excited." He chuckled. "I know you're investigating what happened out at the Cedar farm."

"You do? How do you know that?"

"Your mom told me. Besides, everyone in town is talking about it."

"Okay. What about it?" Beth yawned and stretched out the phone cord to retrieve her coffee cup from the table, take it over to the percolator on the counter, and refill it with coffee.

"I have a load of scrap wood from various projects. And I'm planning to haul it out to the Olson farm, which is just down the road from the Cedars' place. The older Mr. Olson uses it as fuel for their wood-burning furnace in the winter and keeps some of the better pieces for his woodworking projects."

"Really?" Beth suddenly felt more alert.

"Yup. How'd you like to come along and chat with him while I unload it? He hasn't had much to do since he turned over the farming operations to his son. When he isn't sawing boards into shorter boards, he spends his time watching the neighbors. He might have seen something of interest."

"That sounds promising. I'd love to go with you."

"Okay, I'll pick you up in about an hour."

When they got to the Olsons' farm, Beth's dad introduced her, and then he and the younger Mr. Olson left to unload the scrap wood into the Olson's barn. Beth joined old Mr. Olson under a tree in the backyard.

He was seated on a weathered wooden chair next to a pile of wood and a couple of saw horses. She waved away his offer to give her his chair and sat down on one of the tree stumps that served as guest seating.

"I've seen you driving past in that bookmobile. You must be a librarian."

"Yup. Except, right now, I'm just a library assistant. But I'm going to graduate school to become a full-fledged librarian."

"Is that so?"

Mr. Olson leaned forward and picked out a small piece of wood from the pile next to his chair and tossed it onto a pile of similar-sized pieces of wood in a rusty wagon.

"So, when you drove past here, I suppose you were headed over to Jim Thornton's old place?" he asked.

Her dad was right. Old Mr. Olson didn't miss much.

"That's right. They had a bunch of kids staying there and had a hard time making it into town. I got the librarian to okay an extra stop. Only Sunshine and her baby are there now."

"You don't say. Rest of them packed up and left?"

"For the time being. I suppose some of them will be back, especially Sunshine's, um, husband."

He regarded her with amusement, his eyes crinkled nearly shut by years of staring into the sun. "I expect so."

"Meanwhile, her parents are coming for a visit."

"My, my. I'm happy to hear that. They're nice folks. I hope they stop by for a visit while they're here."

"I'll pass that message on to Sunshine the next time I see her," Beth said. "I suppose you remember when the Thorntons sold their farmland to the Cedar family and moved away?"

"Oh, yes." He gazed into the middle distance and frowned. "The Cedars. Now, there's a bunch I won't miss."

"You don't care for the Cedar family."

"I guess I shouldn't speak ill of the dead, but that Vern never had time for anyone but himself. And his dad was the same way."

"So, I gather that you know that Vern passed away."

"Of course. Couldn't miss it, with all the sirens and what not. That's what comes from always being in a hurry—an accident waiting to happen. He should have been more careful."

"So, you think it was an accident."

Mr. Olson paused and stared at her. "So, you think it might *not* have been an accident?"

"The police seem to think so. They arrested a friend of mine. But I'm sure they got the wrong man. I'd like to find out who really did it."

"You don't say?" There was another pause while he sorted through his woodpile and threw chunks into the wagon. "I heard about you. You're that girl who helps solve mysteries, aren't you?"

"Seems like it." Beth laughed. "Maybe I'm just in the wrong place at the wrong time. Did you happen to notice any strangers coming or going around the time of Vern's death, or anything strange going on?"

Mr. Olson stared off into space for a few more moments. "Not then, no. I don't know if you'd say it was strange, but I saw a car passing by, now and then, that I didn't recognize. A sort of sporty, foreign-looking thing."

"What did it look like?"

"It was red and kind of small."

"Do you know where it was going?"

"Not sure if it went there every time it drove past, of course. I saw it pull into the Cedars' driveway one time."

"You did? Did you see who was driving?"

"I didn't get a good look. Nobody from around here, that's for sure."

"Was it a man or a woman?"

"Oh, it was a man. I don't think Vern was home when he passed by."

"I see," Beth said.

He nodded at her with a knowing look. "Maybe it was a coincidence, but I'd see Vern roar past in his pickup truck, then this other fella would pass going the other way."

"When did you see that?"

"Usually on a Friday, in the late afternoon."

"Did that car drive by on the weekend that Vern died?"

"No, not then. I sure would have remembered that." Mr. Olson kicked at the woodpile and dislodged another short piece that he threw into the wagon. "But I saw it other times too. Once it passed by just before you came by in that bookmobile."

Beth suddenly recalled seeing Ruth talking to a man who had his back to the road, as she drove past the Cedars' place. Was that her boyfriend? If so, she was very casual about who saw them together.

"Maybe it was a friend or a relative," she said.

"Could be." Mr. Olson sounded skeptical.

"Thanks for the information. I'm glad you're so observant."

"Glad to help." He smiled bashfully. "You know, some folks think nobody sees what's going on. They don't notice me, I guess. But my eyesight is still pretty sharp, and I notice things. Vernon, the Mrs., and that hired hand, coming and going, even when they shouldn't be, when there's work to do. And then there's the Thornton girl, and God knows who all, coming and going from that place with all their rickety cars. Too many of them. I couldn't keep them all straight."

"Did you notice any of them around the Cedar place the weekend that Vern died?"

"I wouldn't know about that. They're on the other side of his place, so they wouldn't come past here to get to the Cedars' place."

"Oh, sure."

Beth saw her dad heading in their direction. He must have finished unloading the scrap wood.

"Well, thanks again. You've been a big help. Get in touch with my dad if you think of anything else."

"I'll sure do that." Mr. Olson beamed at her.

Beth had her dad drop her at the theater when they got back to Davison City. She wanted to see if Evie needed any help with the scenery and talk over what she'd learned. She walked in the front door, through the lobby, and then into the auditorium. She took a few steps and then froze, her heart beating wildly.

Nigel and Evie were on the stage, talking. His back was turned to her, and she realized, in a flash, that he was the man she'd glimpsed talking to Ruth on her farm.

Evie saw her, raised a hand, and called out, "Hi, Beth."

Nigel turned and waved hello to her too.

Beth forced her feet to move, and she walked toward the stage while her mind churned. What did this mean? Why was Nigel out at the Cedars' place? Was he just there to talk to her about the play? But, how could that be? Mr. Olson said that he'd seen a man driving past numerous times. But maybe it wasn't Nigel. Beth tried to recall what kind of car he drove.

"I just stopped by to see if you needed any help today," Beth said as she walked up the steps from the auditorium onto the stage. Her voice sounded strange to her, and her mouth felt dry.

Evie looked at her more closely. "Are you okay, Beth?"

"Yes. Fine. Just out of breath, I guess. Are you in the middle of something?"

"No, we can finish talking about the scene changes later," Nigel excused himself and went backstage.

Beth waited until he was gone, then stepped close to Evie, grabbed her arm, and said, "We have to talk."

Chapter 27

August 6, 1969

Beth and Evie sat in a booth across the aisle from the Woolworths lunch counter waiting for their lunch order.

"You're acting kind of weird. What's going on?" Evie said.

"I got a shock when I saw Nigel on the stage with you."

"A shock? Why?"

"I suddenly realized it was Nigel who I'd seen out at the Cedar place."

"You saw him out there? When was this?"

"One of the first times that I drove the bookmobile past the Cedar farm. I was thinking about the upcoming radio interview, trying to decide if I should do it. So, I was curious when I passed Vern's place. That's when I saw Ruth standing in the front yard, talking to a man. His back was to the road, so I couldn't see his face, and I didn't realize who he was until just now. When I saw Nigel standing on the stage, facing away from me, I realized he was the man with Ruth that day."

Evie wrinkled her forehead. "Okay, but maybe he just went out there to talk to Ruth about the play. After all, she'd auditioned for a part."

"Yeah, maybe. I could be reading too much into it. But he never said anything about being out there, even after Logan was arrested. And, it had looked to me like he and Ruth were very friendly." Beth told Evie about her visit to the Olson farm, finishing with, "Old Mr. Olson said that he had seen the same small red car going by on a regular basis for some time."

"That *does* sound like Nigel's car," Evie said. "Did Mr. Olson see who was driving the car?"

"No. He just knew it was a man who visited the Cedar farm on a regular basis when Vern wasn't there."

"And you think it might be Nigel?"

"Possibly. That's not a common sort of car around here. And, we suspected Ruth had a boyfriend."

"You should ask your brother about the car," Evie said. "Maybe someone else has a similar car."

"That's a good idea. I'll do that."

The waitress delivered their food, and Beth took a sip of her chocolate malt, reached for the mustard, and spread some on her ham sandwich. Evie picked up her fork and poked at the salad on her diet plate.

"There was another reason I kind of freaked out when I realized it was Nigel I'd seen out there," Beth said. "I thought

Nigel might have put that feather in Logan's desk. After all, he has access to it."

"Yeah, he had the opportunity. But where did he get the feather? And what would be his motive?"

"I don't know. Just to cast blame on Logan, I guess."

"Blame for what? Yes, there was a red feather in Vern's coveralls, and possibly a similar one in Logan's desk. But how does that connect to the murder?" Evie said.

"We keep coming back to that." Beth huffed in frustration. "I feel like there must be a connection, but I can't quite figure it out."

"Yeah, me too. We have a bunch of clues, but no connections. There are the feathers, the threatening notes, the key, and the note that was written on Vern's calendar."

"Right. The note that said 'B 4:30 on Friday, July 11.' That was the day he died, or maybe the day before he died. We still don't know the time of death."

Beth put down her sandwich and stared off into space for a few moments. "According to Mr. Olson, Vern often drove past his place on Friday afternoons. And then he'd see this other guy in the red car drive past, going the other way. Maybe, Vern regularly did something on Fridays at 4:30, so Ruth arranged to have this other fellow come out at that time."

"So, that would mean . . ." Evie speared a piece of lettuce and held it suspended in midair, then pointed it at Beth.

"Maybe Nigel killed Vern so he could have Ruth for himself. Or maybe Vern found out about the affair, maybe by coming home early one Friday afternoon. He got into a fight with Nigel, Nigel accidentally killed Vern, and then tried to make it look like an accident. But, wait, if that's the case, why would he encourage us to investigate? That doesn't make sense."

"You're right. It doesn't. Unless, he was just going along with the idea when the others proposed it, to avoid suspicion. Or, he underestimates us and thinks that we can't really solve the mystery, so he isn't worried."

"Or he *is* innocent," Evie said.

"Let's hope so, for his sake and the sake of the theater. Losing a director is just as bad as losing the owner. We'll have to keep an eye on him and see if he does anything suspicious. If you don't need my help this afternoon, I'm going to talk to a few people."

"No, I don't need you. I'm just working out details of how to arrange things on the stage and move stuff between acts. I need to discuss that with Nigel."

"Great, that will make it easy for you to keep an eye on him."

Evie finished her cottage cheese and started on the square of orange Jell-O. "Who are you going to talk to?"

"My brother, maybe Don Winthrop, and possibly Bill Crample, if I can catch him at the Pig and Whistle after his shift. Want to meet me there?"

"Sure, I'll head over after work," Evie said. "Why do you want to talk to Don?"

"I want to see if I can listen to more tapes of the Red Cedar show. I only listened to the most recent ones. Maybe I missed something important."

"I guess it's worth a try."

"I hope so. We need to find the missing pieces to this puzzle."

They finished their lunches, Beth walked the few blocks from Woolworths to KROW radio station, and found Don in. He was happy to set her up in a sound booth to listen to more tapes. She sorted through them, hoping the labels would provide a clue, but the only information was the name of the show and the date that it aired.

With a sigh, she decided to just listen by date, going back from the time period she'd already covered. She tried to pick out a caller who sounded more threatening or angry than the others, but nothing stood out.

It was a mishmash of topics: sports, politics, new age practices, environmentalism, the war. Pretty much any topic would do, as long as he could disagree with the caller and ridicule them. If the caller agreed with Vern, saying that protestors should be locked up or that environmentalists who wanted to save endangered species were control freaks, he'd cut the call short. Beth guessed verbal brawling was more fun for the listeners than a civil exchange.

After several hours of listening, she began listening to only the beginning and end of each tape in order to get through them faster. Finally, she pushed rewind on the last tape with mixed feelings. She was glad to be done listening to Vern's strident, angry voice but discouraged that she hadn't discovered anything new.

While waiting for the tape to rewind, she decided to call her brother at work and pick his brain about any small red cars he might have seen around town.

"Red sports car, hmm," Gary said. "I can't say that we've had one in the shop. I don't have the right tools."

"They require different tools? Why's that?"

"Different sizes. They use the metric system over there."

"Oh, sure. So, have you seen any around town?"

"I suppose this is for your investigation."

"Is that common knowledge?"

"I'm afraid so. You solve a couple mysteries, and folks start to expect it. I'll have to start calling you Miss Marple. Let me think, little red cars. Well, there's that theater guy, the director. What's his name?"

"Nigel," Beth said with a sinking feeling.

"Yeah, him. There's a red VW Beetle I've seen around town. Let me think. Yeah, it belongs to the lady who runs the candy store. I have no idea where she gets it serviced. Maybe in Grand Bend. Let me think if there are any others."

Beth started to rummage in the drawers of the desk for a pad and pencil to make notes. She found a stash of miscellaneous pens and worn pencils in the top drawer and a square memo pad.

"Oh, my goodness!" she exclaimed as she pulled it out of the drawer.

"What? What happened?"

"Nothing. I just found something interesting." Beth paused, examining it. "If you think of any other little red cars, let me know. I've got to go now. Talk to you later."

Beth rushed out of the sound booth and through the open door into Don's office. He was on the phone. He looked up, surprised to see her burst in on him.

"Think about it and get back to me if you decide to go ahead with those ads. It's a great deal and should really increase your sales," he said and then ended the call. "What is it, Beth?"

"This pad." She held it out to him. "Where did you get it?"

"You seem pretty excited about a notepad," he said. "What's so special about it?"

"The shape. I've been looking for ones like this, but I couldn't find them. They don't sell them in any of the stores in town, as far as I know."

Don looked puzzled. "I don't know. Our receptionist orders supplies. I suppose she ordered them. There's a box of them in the storeroom."

"Everyone at the radio station has these?" Beth asked.

"Yes, that's right," Don said.

"Do you mind if I hang onto this one?" Beth asked.

"Not at all. We have plenty. Did you finish listening to the tapes?"

"Oh, yeah. Thanks for your help," Beth said. "I guess I'll be going now."

She gathered up her things and slipped the notepad into her purse.

Chapter 28

August 6, 1969

Beth took her favorite booth in the back corner of the Pig and Whistle where she could keep an eye on who came through the door. The booth was separate from the others. And, between the music coming from the jukebox and the hum and click of the off-kilter ceiling fan, Beth was pretty certain any conversation she had there wasn't overheard.

Soon, Evie joined her. They ordered beers, and the frosty mugs formed puddles of condensation on the table between them.

"How did it go this afternoon?" Evie asked.

"It was very interesting." Beth dug around in her purse, retrieved the notepad, and handed it across the table to Evie.

Evie's eyes widened. "Wow! Where did you get this?"

"From the radio station." Beth related how she had found the notepad. "Apparently, they have a box full of these in their storeroom."

"That's wild." Evie handed the pad back to Beth, who stashed it back in her purse. "So, anyone at the radio station could have sent the notes as a joke or just to freak Vern out if they had something on him or didn't like him."

"Which covers almost everyone, except management and sales. I suppose they liked him well enough because he was bringing in a good-sized audience."

"One thing is odd." Evie paused and took a sip of beer. "Wouldn't Vern have known from the size and shape of the notes that they came from the radio station?"

"I suppose so. But maybe he was trying to figure out who sent them or why. Maybe that's why he had one of the notes in the pocket of his overalls on the day he died."

"Or, he had just gotten that one."

"That's possible. Anyway, it seems unlikely that someone from the radio would go out to Vern's place and kill him by knocking him over the head in a grain bin. So, I think the notes are probably unrelated to the murder, don't you?"

"Yeah. They were probably just a joke or a warning to stop doing something. Maybe to stop stealing office supplies." Evie laughed.

"That sounds about right," Beth said. "How about you? Did you catch Nigel doing anything suspicious?"

"Not a thing. If he's guilty, he's doing an excellent job of hiding it," Evie said. "Did you talk to your brother?"

"Yeah. I asked him about small red cars. The only two he could think of offhand were Nigel's sports car and the VW Bug that the candy lady drives. I think we can safely eliminate her from our list of suspects." Beth laughed.

The screen door slammed shut as Bill Crample entered the bar. He glanced in their direction, quickly looked away, and headed to the bar.

Beth leaned toward Evie and said in low tones, "He's ignoring us."

"We can't have that." Evie's eyes danced mischievously. "Bill. Oh, Bill," she called out, waved, and flashed a bright smile. "Come over and join us."

He lifted a finger in resigned acknowledgement. When he got the beer he ordered, he picked it up and strolled over.

Beth scooted over and patted the bench next to her. "Join us."

"Ladies." He nodded to them. "I can't stay long," he said as he sat down.

"We're happy for any time you can spare," Beth said.

"What are you two up to?"

"Just enjoying a little refreshment on a hot day. How about you?" Evie asked and favored him with another dazzling smile.

"Right." He regarded them with narrowed eyes. "If there was one more member in your group, it could be a coven," he said.

"Is that a reference to the three witches in *Macbeth*? I'm impressed," Beth said.

"Glad to hear it," he said.

"We were wondering if you could help us out just a teensy bit," Evie said with a vivid smile.

"Ah ha! As I thought, this is an ambush." He took a long pull of beer.

"No, it's not. We just haven't heard if they established Vern's time of death," Beth said. "Has that been determined?"

"I'm not the investigating officer. You'd have to ask Captain Swenson about that."

"But we're not friends with him. We are friends with you. And you *are* involved," Beth said. "After all, you went out to Vern's place to collect evidence. By the way, did I ever thank you for including us on that little jaunt?"

"Nope. Can't say you did. As I recall, you left in a huff."

"After you told us to take a hike? Yeah, I guess I did. Sorry about that. But, thanks for including us in the first place."

"You're welcome," he mumbled and then stared into his beer.

"So, how about it? What's the harm in sharing that information?" Beth persisted.

Bill sighed. "It has to remain confidential."

"Oh, it will," Beth said.

"Our lips are sealed," Evie said.

Bill looked from one to the other, as though trying to gauge their sincerity. He sighed again and then shrugged. "Sometime on Saturday. They couldn't be sure of a more exact time. The heat in the grain bin changed things, but it was probably Saturday afternoon. It seems his last meal was a cheese sandwich and chips, so maybe sometime after lunch."

"Okay. So, Saturday afternoon. That's what we thought," Beth said. "Thanks."

Bill grunted an acknowledgement, then quickly finished his beer and said goodbye.

After he left, Beth said, "So, the noise the hippies heard over there on Friday night most likely was Vern doing some work around the place. And then something happened the next day."

"Or, what happened on Friday precipitated the murder," Evie said. "There was something scheduled for that Friday at 4:30, remember?"

"Yeah. And, it was a regular occurrence, according to Mr. Olson."

"I wonder why Vern wrote it on the calendar if it was a regular appointment," Evie said. "Maybe it was at a different time than usual."

"Good point. I need to talk to Mr. Olson again to see if that was the case and to see if someone is still passing by the Olson farm every Friday afternoon. If so, we should try to follow them and figure out what's going on. What are you doing on Friday afternoon?"

"It sounds like I might be staking out the Cedars' farm with you," Evie said.

"Another good idea," Beth said.

They ordered another round of drinks and started planning.

Chapter 29

August 8, 1969

Beth and Evie sat in Beth's car in Mr. Olson's driveway, partially hidden behind a row of windbreaker trees that lined the road. They watched through curtains of rain coursing down the windshield for the red car to pass. Periodically, as the car windows fogged up, Beth pulled down the cuff of her sweater from under her rain jacket and used it to clear a porthole. Evie did the same on her side.

The rain had rolled in early that morning, at least temporarily ending the heat wave. All day long, huge banks of cumulus clouds rumbled across the dome of the sky, lightning streaked, thunder boomed, and rain poured down. As they waited, Beth watched the wheat flatten and then spring back up as the wind raked the field across the road.

Mr. Olson had given them permission to be there when Beth had called to ask him some follow-up questions. Although he'd seemed surprised to hear from her, he'd freely answered her questions. It seemed to her that he enjoyed the attention.

He said that, yes, the red car was still passing by on Friday afternoons. And, on the Friday before Vern's death, it might have passed by earlier than usual, which supported their suspicion that Vern's regular Friday routine had been changed for that day. But, Mr. Olson said, he wasn't sure because he didn't wear a watch and hadn't tracked the exact times the car had driven past.

Since they didn't know when to expect the car, they'd come out early and had been sitting here for over an hour. Beth glanced at her watch, wondering if they might have missed the car or if it wasn't coming today.

Just then, Evie said, "There it goes." She pointed at a red sports car that streaked past.

Beth glanced at her watch again. It was 3:45.

"Let's see where it goes," Beth said.

They were out on the road in time to see the car turn into the Cedars' driveway. As they drove slowly past, they saw it pull into the barn.

"Now what?" Evie asked.

"Well, we can't follow him into the barn. I guess we'll go back to our lookout spot and watch for him to drive the other way," Beth said.

She used the pull-off in front of the hippie's mailbox, where she parked the bookmobile on Mondays, to do a U-turn, noticing that they had a new mailbox. Sunshine's parents must be visiting and helping with repairs.

Within fifteen minutes of parking back in their lookout spot, the red car streaked past again, going the other way.

"That was quick," Beth said as she started the car and followed him. "I'm guessing he wasn't there for a romantic encounter with Ruth."

"Don't lose him," Evie said.

"I'll do my best," Beth said. She stomped on the accelerator, and her old car lumbered forward, spraying gravel and water from puddles forming on the road behind her.

The red car sped up, slowing only to make the turn onto the highway, where it turned west. By the time Beth followed it onto the highway, it was far ahead of them.

"Luckily it's a high-visibility color car," Beth said.

She accelerated and her car started to hydroplane and swerve. A lightning flash, closely followed by a boom of thunder, made them both jump and then laugh.

"I think that's our cue to slow down," Beth said, easing off the accelerator.

"Do you think he knows we're following him?" Evie asked.

"Maybe. Or maybe he always drives fast. If you drive a red sports car, you probably like going fast. Luckily, my black car doesn't stand out in this weather."

"I bet he's heading to Grand Bend."

"That would be my guess too. I'll back off in case he spotted us. He'll have to slow down once he gets to the city."

They soon lost sight of the red car. But, as they approached the smokestacks of the sugar beet plant on the edge of town, they spotted it waiting at a stop light. Beth slowed some more, allowing a couple cars to move in between them and the red car.

When the light changed, they followed at a discrete distance as he turned into a side street on the outskirts of town. Now, there was no one else between their cars. Beth hoped they weren't too obvious.

The red car pulled into a driveway. As Beth drove past it, she tried to get a glimpse of the driver, but his windows were fogged up, and so were theirs.

"Where was it that he turned in?" Beth asked.

Evie craned her head to look behind them. "It looks like it's a storage facility."

"Really? Okay. I guess I'll drive around the block."

"Hang on. Take the alley." Evie pointed. "Maybe there's another way in."

"Good idea." Beth turned.

She slowly drove along the back of the long metal building until they came to a large dumpster on the side of the building and a rutted gravel driveway leading up to it. She parked next to the dumpster.

"I'm going to see what's going on," Beth said as she pulled up the hood on her rain jacket. "You coming?"

"Why not." Evie bit her bottom lip and then grinned.

They quietly got out of the car, crept around the edge of the dumpster, and leaned forward. Beth watched as a man stepped out of the red car and circled around to his trunk. He looked around. As he did, she got a clear view of his face. She gasped and they both ducked back.

"Did you see that?" Beth whispered. "That's Nigel."

Evie nodded, her eyes wide.

They peeked around the edge of the dumpster again and watched as he removed a couple of medium-sized cardboard boxes from his trunk, carried them into the storage unit, and then quickly came out, locked it, closed the car trunk, and drove off.

"Now what?" Evie asked.

"Let's get out of the rain," Beth said.

They hurried back to the car and jumped in. Water dripped down from Beth's bangs; she swiped it away with the damp cuff of her sweater.

"It *was* Nigel!" Evie said. "We thought it might be. But I didn't want to believe it. I wonder what he's up to."

"Whatever it is, it's not just an affair," Beth said. "It must be something illegal. Did you see the way he looked around before he took the boxes out of his trunk?"

"Yeah, I did. Do you think it has anything to do with Vern's death?"

"I hope not," Beth said. "We'd know more if we knew what was in those boxes."

Beth started the car and slowly drove to the storage unit where Nigel had been and parked.

"Wait here. I'm just going to check the lock." Beth hopped out, ran over to the lock, took a close look at it, and rattled it to be sure it was locked, and then ran back to the car.

"It's padlocked. That's probably what the key opens."

"You mean the one in Vern's desk?"

"Yup."

"Too bad we didn't keep it."

"Yeah, too bad." Beth paused. "Well, it wouldn't be hard to break in. We could get a bolt cutter or a crowbar from a hardware store. If we do that, we should do it after dark," Beth said.

"Or, we could just ask Ruth to borrow the key."

"No, we can't do that. Whatever is going on, Ruth must be involved too, unless she's completely clueless."

"So, you'd rather break in?"

"I don't want to. That will broadcast the fact that someone's been snooping, and we'd be the likely suspects."

"So, what should we do?"

"Right now, we'll stake out this place and see if anyone picks up whatever Nigel put in there and come up with a plan for later."

Beth reversed the car, drove down to the end of the block and parked where they could keep watch. To pass the time, they talked while they shelled and ate peanuts while rain drummed on the roof of her car. The rain started to let up after a couple hours. Then, a dark-colored van drove past.

"Try to see the license plate," Beth said as she frantically cranked down the window and leaned out.

The car slowed down and turned into the driveway of the storage facility.

"Did you see it?" Beth asked.

"No, it went by too fast."

"Wait here and see if you can catch it when he comes out. I'm going to see if I can get a better look."

Beth ran down the block, stopping next to the edge of the driveway, and leaned forward.

The van had stopped in front of the same storage unit. The driver, a man in a dark jacket, got out, unlocked the padlock, pulled up the sliding door, and went inside.

Beth ran to the van and crouched down behind it. She took a close look at the license plate. It had the outline of a bison on the bottom, next to a metal date plate that read "Manitoba, 1969." She tried to memorize the number, repeating it to herself several times. It was two letters followed by three numbers, KG 344. Although, she doubted that Bill Crample would be able to look up a Canadian license plate number.

She heard footsteps on the other side of the van and tiptoed around to the front. She heard the driver open the cargo doors on the back of the van, push boxes in, and then start walking back toward the storage unit.

Beth tiptoed back around to the rear of the van and peeked inside. There were a few cardboard boxes inside with the logos A-1 Crafts and Beads.

This was too weird. Beth stood there, lost in thought for a moment. Why would anyone be so secretive about craft materials?

The driver came around the back of the van, carrying another armload of boxes.

"Hey you! What are you doing here?" he asked with a fierce scowl on his weather-beaten face.

"Who, me?" Beth forced a smile. "I was just walking past, taking a shortcut, and I noticed the boxes. I always wondered what people put in these storage units. So, you sell craft supplies?"

His eyes narrowed in suspicion. "Shortcut to where?"

"Oh, I live just down the street." Beth gestured vaguely. "I was out for a walk."

"In this weather?" He took two steps toward her. She could smell tobacco and alcohol on his breath.

"Yes, well, I'm trying to get more exercise. It's good for your health, you know." She retreated a few steps.

"So is minding your own business." He slammed the van's cargo doors shut and continued to stare at her.

"Well, yes, I suppose that's true. Anyway, I can see you're busy. I'll be going now," she said as she backed away. She turned and ran back to the car and jumped into the driver's side, panting.

"What happened? Did you get the license plate number?" Evie asked.

"Yeah, and I got caught doing it. Let's get out of here," Beth put the car in gear and drove off, making several turns, while watching in the rearview mirror to be sure she wasn't being followed. When she was sure, she pulled over to the side of the street and explained what happened.

"It was a Manitoba license plate. Write it down."

Evie retrieved a small notebook and a pen from her purse.

"I think the number was KG 344. I don't know what's in those boxes, but whatever it is, it's not just craft supplies."

Beth and Evie discussed their options. Now that the van driver had gotten a good look at Beth, he could give a good description to Ruth or anyone else involved. They decided that there was no point being too subtle.

"We can either pry or cut the lock off of the storage unit door or get the key from Vern's desk with or without Ruth's knowledge," Beth concluded. "First, let's take a closer look at that lock."

Beth drove up to the storage unit and parked in front of it. She noticed that there was a letter 'B' painted on the door. By this time, the rain storm had passed, and it was just drizzling.

"I really should learn to pick a lock," Beth said.

"Not a typical skill for a librarian." Evie chuckled.

"No, but it would be a useful one for me. These mysteries seem to keep falling into my lap. I wonder if the universe is trying to tell me something."

Beth stared at the lock for a moment. "Hang on." She got out and examined it.

When she returned to the car, she said, "It's not exactly Fort Knox. I think all I need to do is unscrew the hinge from the doorframe."

"That sounds good. And, if we can do that without getting charged with breaking and entering, maybe we can stay out of jail. As much as I like Logan, I don't want to keep him company. Do you have a screwdriver?"

"I'm not sure. See what you can find in the glove box. I'll check the trunk. My dad or brother might have put one in the car."

Evie was digging through the over-filled glove box when Beth reappeared outside of her window. "Eureka," she said, brandishing a large flat-head screwdriver.

Beth headed to the hinge, and Evie got out of the car and followed her.

"Damn, it's a Phillips-head screw," Beth said. "I hope I can make it work. What is the saying, lefty loosey, righty tighty?"

"Yup. But be careful. Don't strip it."

Beth tilted the screwdriver and gingerly worked at turning the screw. After a few tries, she loosened it enough to finish unscrewing it with her fingers and then set to work on the bottom one. Soon, she'd detached the hinge. Then, they pulled up the door and went inside.

A row of cardboard boxes sat on the metal shelving units that lined the walls. They were labeled Terraform Craft Supplies, Inc.

"These have different labels than the ones that the van driver took," Beth said. "Those said A-1 Crafts and Beads. Maybe they're going to different places."

Beth pulled a box off one of the shelves, put it on the floor, and opened it. "This stuff doesn't look too valuable." She held up handfuls of bagged beads and feathers.

Evie picked up a bag. "Yeah. If it *is* valuable, why would they leave it in a storage unit that's so easy to break into?"

"I don't know. Maybe because it's near the highway and it wouldn't be here for long. It was just a short time from when Nigel just dropped off some boxes until the van picked some up. Which means, someone may be coming to get these soon."

Evie held the small bag of shiny red stones up to the light coming in from outside, tilting and squinting at it for a better look. "It just looks like craft supplies to me. But maybe there are drugs hidden in some of these bags. Or some of these beads are really precious stones."

"Well, we can't stick around here and figure it out," Beth said. "Put that box in the car. I'll secure this place before we're caught red-handed. If they *are* just craft supplies, we'll put it all back, hopefully before anyone knows it's missing."

Evie stashed the box in the back seat of the car, while Beth closed the storage unit door and screwed the hinge back in place, leaving it slightly loose for easier access when they returned. Then, she picked up a pinch of mud and rubbed it on the hinge and screws to hide the scratch marks.

Beth drove around the block and parked where they could keep watch. Then, they got out of the front of the car, and climbed into the backseat with the box between them, and started pulling out the contents. There were glass and plastic beads in a rainbow of colors, wires, thread, hooks, and assorted crafting supplies. They examined all the various-sized packages of beads. They were all sealed shut and didn't seem to contain anything except what was on the labels.

"If there's anything suspicious here, I'm sure not seeing it," Evie said.

"Me neither. But if it's all innocent, why was the van driver acting so weird? He sure seemed angry about being seen," Beth said.

Near the bottom of the box, Beth found a large plastic bag marked "Assorted Feathers." She picked it up and shook it, rearranging the feathers.

"Look at these." She handed the bag across to Evie. "Aren't those red ones like the one we found in Logan's desk?"

Evie examined it. "Could be. Yeah."

"Okay, then. I think I know what this is all about."

"Do you mean it's about feathers?"

"Yeah. I think so. Crazy, I know. I'll explain later."

Beth shoved the plastic bag full of feathers under the driver's seat and started throwing the rest of the craft supplies back into the box.

"Can you finish repacking this stuff? I'm going to drive to the nearest drugstore and buy some packing tape. Then, we can tape up this box and put it back where it came from."

A frantic fifteen minutes later, they had returned the box to its spot on the shelf and resecured the door of the storage unit. Beth dropped the screwdriver into her purse. And then they started back to Davison City.

A beautiful rainbow arched across the western sky. The waving grain in the field below the rainbow glistened with drying raindrops. Beth tuned the radio to the top 100 station, and "Good Morning Starshine" came on.

"The perfect song for the occasion." Beth gestured at the scenery.

"I'm glad you're in such a good mood," Evie said. "But tell me already, what is this all about?"

"Okay. Remember how Mr. Nobis confiscated the feather we found in Logan's desk because he said it was an eagle feather, and it was illegal for us to have it?"

"Yeah."

"And the delivery van that came to pick up the boxes today had Canadian license plates?"

"Right."

"Well, there's probably some kind of international black market for eagle feathers. When something is illegal, and people want it, they find a way to get it. And that drives up the price."

"Oh . . ." Evie said slowly. "So, you're saying that Vern was involved in some sort of eagle feather smuggling ring, along with Ruth and Nigel?"

"It would appear so."

"And, someone who collected the feathers painted them red and then hid them among other feathers and put them in boxes with other craft supplies to hide them?"

"Bingo."

"Wow." Evie sat, humming along with the song for a few moments. "Do you think that's why Vern was killed?"

"Possibly. The threatening notes could have been from a blackmailer who figured out what was going on."

"Hmm. Maybe. But is there enough money involved in this trade to make it worth blackmail and murder? If so, how can we prove it and get Logan out of jail?

"You ask good questions," Beth said.

"Do you think we should show the bag of feathers to Mr. Nobis and see what he thinks?"

Beth grimaced. "I don't know. He seemed pretty angry about our so-called tampering with evidence when he saw one feather. I'm not sure I want to explain how we got a whole bag full of feathers."

"Then, what should we do?"

Beth drummed her fingers on the steering wheel and bit her bottom lip while she thought. Then she exclaimed, "I've got it! I'll talk to Mr. Flack. He's always looking for a good story. An international smuggling ring, maybe connected with blackmail and murder? It doesn't get much juicier than that. What do you think?"

"That's a great idea. That would make us confidential sources. He could get the evidence to the police without involving us."

"This calls for a celebration," Beth said. "Beer and burgers?"

"That's another great idea." Evie laughed.

Chapter 30

August 8, 1969

Beth and Evie sat across the desk from Mr. Nobis. "I'm sorry, but I don't think this is quite as significant as you might have hoped," he said. He picked up the bag of feathers and shook it. "While you may be correct that eagle feathers are being smuggled across the Canadian border, if caught, the perpetrators would face fines and perhaps some jail time. But I doubt that it rises to the level of motivation for murder. There must be more to it than that." He smiled apologetically at them.

Beth felt hope draining out of her and heaviness settling in. She had been so sure that this was a major break in the case. "Are you sure?" she asked.

"Well, no. One can't say for sure what anyone might do under duress. But it does seem unlikely. Tell you what, I'll pass this evidence on to the pertinent authorities. If they make an arrest, it would make an interesting bit of local news. I'll let you know if anything develops."

They thanked him for his time and left.

"Do you still feel like stopping for a hamburger and beer?" Beth asked.

"Not really," Evie said. "How about you?"

"No. Suddenly, I'm really tired. I just want to go home and take a nap. It seems like we wasted the day and broke into the storage unit for no good reason. I guess I'll see you tomorrow at the theater."

"Sure. See you then."

When Beth got home, she kicked off her shoes and padded around the kitchen, making a bologna sandwich and putting the kettle on for tea. Chestnut followed her around, meowing.

"Yes, I know, meow to you too. Did you miss me, or do you just want your kibbles?" She got the box out of the cupboard and poured some into his dish.

He settled down and crunched happily.

"It doesn't take much to make you happy, does it?"

He looked at her and said, "Meow."

"Lucky you."

Beth sat at the kitchen table with her sandwich, waiting for the teakettle to boil. She realized she'd hardly had a thing to eat since breakfast as she wolfed down her sandwich while sorting through the mail that had piled up in the wire basket on the table. She made three piles: open now, look at later, and throw out.

She picked up a plain, business-sized envelope with her name and address typed on it. There was no return address. She looked at the postmark, wondering which pile to put it in. It was from Davison City and dated over a week ago. Still undecided, she ripped it open, and a small, folded piece of paper dropped out. She picked it up, with a tingling feeling on the back of her neck, and unfolded it. It was the same size as the notepad she'd gotten from the radio station. Printed in block, capital letters, the note read, "SNOOPY GIRLS BEWARE. CURIOSITY KILLED THE CAT."

She stared at it, her heart beating faster, then dropped it on the table, rushed to the phone, and called Evie.

"Evie? I got one of those notes in the mail."

"Notes? What notes?"

"A threatening note. You know, like the ones Vern was getting. Can you come over?"

"I'll be right there."

The teakettle started to whistle just as she hung up the phone. She jumped and emitted a small scream. Chestnut jumped too. Then he looked at her with narrowed eyes, as though annoyed, before turning back to his supper.

"You're right. I need to get a grip."

Beth turned off the teakettle and put a box of tea bags and a couple of mugs and spoons on the kitchen counter. A few minutes later there was a knock on her front door.

Beth rushed to the door. "That was quick," she said as she opened the door. "Oh, it's you."

Bill Crample, wearing his uniform, stood in her doorway.

"You sound so excited to see me," he said.

"Sorry, I was expecting Evie. She's on her way over." Beth leaned around him and looked down the street for Evie's car. "What can I do for you? You're not going to invite us along to collect another clue, are you?"

"No, nothing like that." He looked at his shoes and fell silent.

Evie's car pulled up and parked behind Bill's squad car.

Evie waved to them as she got out. "Did he tell you?" she called out as she approached the house.

"Tell me what?" Beth asked when Evie got up to the door.

"On my way over, I saw Bill coming out of the bank. He asked what was new and I mentioned the note."

Beth felt a little annoyed. Why had Evie told Bill that? And how had he gotten here before Evie? Had he run through red lights?

"I guess you both better come in, then." Beth stepped back, waved them in, and closed the door behind them. "Come through to the kitchen. I was just making some tea."

They followed her. "Have a seat." She gestured toward the table, scooped up the mail, and dumped it back into the wire basket.

Bill and Evie sat down at the small kitchen table. Bill removed his hat and dropped it on the table. Chestnut stopped eating and sniffed around the visitors' legs and rubbed up against them while they petted him and said hello.

"Is this the note?" Evie asked, picking it up and reading it. "Wow! That *is* scary. Isn't it?"

"Yeah, kind of. Unless it's just a joke."

Evie handed it to Bill, who held it gingerly by the edges and then put it down on the table.

Beth squeezed around them as she retrieved an extra mug and spoon and a package of cookies from the cupboard. She put some cookies on a plate. Then she put the plate and the tea-making supplies in the middle of the table and sat down with them.

"When did you get this?" Bill pointed at the note.

"I'm not sure," Beth said. "My mail has been piling up."

"So I see," he said, looking at the overflowing basket.

Beth picked the envelope that the note had come in out of the basket and looked at the postmark. "It was sent July 30th."

"Be careful," Bill said. "There might be prints on that envelope."

"Okay."

"So, that was after we were at the radio station," Evie said. "Maybe someone at the radio station sent it as a joke."

"Unlikely," Bill said. "Once Vern was dead, the joke, if that's what it was, was over. I can't see any of those guys thinking it was funny to send threatening notes to a . . ." He trailed off.

"To who? An innocent girl?" Beth batted her eyes at him.

"Yeah, something like that," Bill said, his blue eyes crinkling in amusement.

"Male chauvinism aside, I agree," Beth said. "The radio night crew might have come up with a stupid stunt like sending threatening notes to Vern, just to freak him out. But, as Bill said, once he was dead, the joke was over."

"Then what is it?" Evie asked.

"Probably, what it seems to be," Bill said. "A threat from someone who doesn't want you snooping around."

"Like the killer," Beth said.

"Could be," Bill said. "Or at least someone with something to hide. I warned you not to get involved."

Beth scowled at him. "Did you? Well, that's water under the bridge. We *are* involved until Logan is cleared. By the way, when is he getting bailed out?"

"After he has his bail hearing and arranges bail," Bill said.

"Okay. So, what's taking so long?" Beth asked.

"Not sure. I think the judge has been out sick. Ask his lawyer. I understand you two are pretty chummy."

"We are not chummy. Is it being chummy to talk to people?" Beth asked.

"No. But he's . . . I mean, he's not . . . Never mind. Umm, I'd better get going. I'm still on duty. I'll take that note and the envelope." He held out his hand.

"Why?"

"I could dust it for prints. Although, now that we've all handled it, any prints that were on it are probably too smudged to be useful."

"Oh, all right." Beth reluctantly gave him the envelope and the note.

"And, for God's sake, be careful," he said and then left.

After he'd closed the door, Evie said, "You have a way of reducing him to stuttering."

"I wish you hadn't told him about the note," Beth said.

"I'm sorry. It just sort of slipped out."

"Yeah, I know." Beth sighed. "I just get tired of his hovering. Imagine! He must have rushed over here like a bat out of hell."

"But he can be useful, occasionally."

Chapter 31

August 11, 1969

Beth was up early to restock the bookmobile before heading out on her route. She was carrying an armload of books out of the back door of the library when Bill Crample pulled up in his squad car. He parked and jumped out.

"Need help with that?" He held out his hands.

"Sure. Thanks." She handed him the stack of books and climbed into the bookmobile. Bill followed her. "Put them down there." She indicated the small table behind the driver's seat. "What brings you around here so bright and early? You look like you have news."

"Yup. Logan's bail hearing is scheduled for this morning. If his lawyer can arrange bail, he'll be out of jail sometime this afternoon."

Beth spun around. "No kidding? That's great!"

"I thought you might like to know that."

"I do! Who else knows? Does Evie know?"

"His lawyer probably knows. But, you're the first one I've told."

"Thanks, Bill. That is such great news! What has it been, over three weeks since he was, um, detained?"

"Since I arrested him, you mean?"

"Yeah, that. I know. You were just doing your job. Oh, this is so great. I'm going to call Evie and let her know. That's all right, isn't it?"

"Sure. Why not?" he said with a crooked smile.

"Great. She'll be so excited. Everyone at the theater will be." Beth paused. "So, you don't care who I tell?"

He looked at her with narrowed eyes. "Who do you have in mind?"

"Well, I'm driving past Ruth's farm this morning. She probably will be happy to know that the show will go on as scheduled."

"Maybe you'd better leave her alone."

"Leave her alone, why?"

"You don't need to poke your nose into her business."

Beth's good mood faded. She stared stonily at him, trying not to react. Deciding that she didn't have time to argue, she forced a smile. "Yeah, maybe you're right. Anyway, I'd better get going. And, I'm sure you have places to be."

He frowned. Without another word, he turned, strode back to his squad car, and drove off. Beth hurried into the library to call Evie.

"That is wonderful." Evie sounded even more excited than Beth was. "You're driving the bookmobile today. Right?"

"Yeah. I wish I could be there when Logan gets released, but I guess I can't be."

"Tell you what, I'll call his lawyer and ask him to let me know what happens today. Swing by the theater when you get back to town, and I'll give you an update. If Logan feels up to it, maybe we can go out and celebrate this evening."

"Sounds good. See you then."

Her first stop was the church's parking lot in Plato. While there, Beth kept checking her watch as a few people stopped by to return books and browse for new ones to check out. Would this day never end? She couldn't wait to finish her route and get back to town. She finally might get to talk to Logan and ask him what he knew about Vern's death and why he'd been arrested. What questions had the police asked him, she wondered.

At last, it was almost time to go. Beth cleared her throat and looked at her watch to hurry along a lingering library patron. They took the hint and brought their books to be checked out. Then, Beth packed up and set off to her next stop, which was the hippie farm.

Beth slowed as she drew near the Cedar farm, debating if she should stop in or not. Maybe Ruth already had heard about

Logan's bail hearing. Even if she hadn't, maybe Bill was right and she should steer clear. Had Ruth said something to him about resenting Beth's investigation into Vern's death? Anyway, what more could she learn from talking to Ruth? She had an alibi. She had been in the cities when Vern died, so she was no longer a suspect.

On the other hand, Ruth must know something about the eagle feather smuggling, since it hadn't stopped after Vern's death. But, how could she approach her about that? Maybe it was better if she didn't mention it.

Beth was about to drive past when she saw Ruth coming out of the house carrying a suitcase and heading towards her car. A young man jumped out of the driver's side and opened the trunk of the car. It took Beth a second to recognize him. It was Lester, Sunshine's boyfriend! What was he doing here? Where were the two of them going? Consumed with curiosity, Beth forgot her scruples and turned into their driveway. She parked the bookmobile and jumped out.

She waved to the two of them as she headed in their direction. They stopped, frozen for a second, staring at her. "Hi, Lester. I see you're back. What are you doing here?" Beth called out.

He gaped at her, slammed the trunk shut, and walked towards her. Ruth followed him.

"Hi, Beth. What brings you here?" Ruth asked.

"Oh right, Beth," Lester said. "The library lady."

"That's me," Beth said. "It looks like you're planning a trip. Are you going together?"

"Yes, we are." Ruth put her hands on her hips. "Why do you ask?"

"Just wondering. I haven't seen Lester for a while. I was under the impression that he went out east for a music festival."

"That's right," Lester said. "I came back to get Ruth. We're going back together."

"You and Ruth? What about Sunshine and your son?"

"That's over. I won't be tied down," he said.

"I see." Beth stared at him with disgust, noticing his weak chin and the shifty eyes. What kind of man would abandon his family with such a cavalier attitude?

"You should mind your own business," Ruth said to Beth.

"Yeah, I suppose you're right." Beth paused. "I just stopped by to tell you that Logan has his bail hearing this morning and will probably get out of jail afterwards. I thought you might like to know that the show will go on as scheduled."

"Hurrah for the show," Ruth said. "But I won't be here."

"So, you're not planning to come back?" Beth asked.

"Not anytime soon. I'm done being stuck at the edge of nowhere. We're going to New York City after the music festival. Maybe I'll be in a Broadway show someday."

"And, the farm? What will happen to it?"

"I'm putting it up for sale."

"And the smuggling business, what about that?"

Ruth's face flushed a bright red.

"The what?" Lester's mouth dropped open, and he stared at Ruth.

"I don't know what she's talking about," Ruth said. "Be a dear, and get those suitcases from my bedroom."

Lester stopped for a moment, staring at Beth and then Ruth.

"Go on," Ruth said. "We should get going."

He huffed, then turned and walked into the house.

"What's that you were saying? Something about smuggling?"

"Don't play dumb. We know all about the eagle feather smuggling."

Ruth laughed. "The what? Feather smuggling? You must be kidding."

"Not at all. My friend Evie and I have been investigating. We followed Nigel from here to a storage unit in Grand Bend and discovered what was going on."

"Is that so? Well, I don't know anything about it." Ruth dug in her purse, pulled out a pack of cigarettes and a lighter, and lit one. "Either you're making it up, or Nigel had something going with Vern. But it didn't involve me."

Beth scrutinized Ruth as she stood. tapping one foot impatiently and smoking. Either she was a good actress, or she was telling the truth. She'd see if she could rattle her a bit.

"Aren't you and Nigel lovers?" Beth asked.

Ruth stopped, her cigarette suspended in midair, and glared at Beth. "No, we're not *lovers*. We had a brief fling. Nigel and I used to meet up in the cities from time to time. And I let him buy me things. But, when he followed me up here, that was just too much. Frankly, he wasn't man enough for me. I need a younger, more virile man."

"Like Lester?"

"Exactly."

Beth laughed.

"So why was Nigel coming out here every Friday afternoon, while Vern was away on business?"

"You'll have to ask him about that." Ruth threw down her cigarette butt and ground it with the toe of her sandal. "He became buddies with Vern, I guess. I never paid any attention to what they did together."

Lester came out of the house carrying two more suitcases and put them in the trunk.

"Come on, Lester," Ruth said. "Let's get going."

Ruth climbed into the passenger seat of the car and slammed the car door behind her.

"Yeah, Lester, you'd better do what you're told," Beth said.

"Up yours," he said. He jumped into the driver's seat of the car and revved the motor.

Beth got back into the driver's seat in the bookmobile and watched as they drove past, making a note of the license plate number, just in case.

Once they were gone, Beth headed down the road to the hippie farm and parked next to the new mailbox. She honked the horn and then hopped out. Then, she slid open the side door of the van and put down the step stool. The farm dogs raced down the driveway, barking. Then wagged their tails when they realized it was a friend.

A grain truck rumbled up on the gravel road and stopped next to the bookmobile. Dave, the Cedars' hired had, leaned out the window.

"Hello there," he called out.

Beth climbed back into the driver's seat and rolled down her window to talk to him.

"Hi, Dave. Still hard at work, I see."

"Yup. I'm not sure what will become of the farm. But no sense letting the grain sit in the field, I guess."

"I suppose not. I just talked to Ruth. She was heading out. Not sure when she'll be back."

"Is that so? That puts another wrinkle into things, doesn't it?"

"I bet it does."

"Anyway. Are you still looking into Vern's death?"

"Yes, I am. But I'm not getting too far with it. As a matter of fact, Logan is getting out on bail today. At least, I hope it's today. I'm hoping he knows something that might help."

Dave stared off into the distance while he took a toothpick out of the chest pocket of his coveralls and inserted it into his mouth. "'Bout that. I was wondering if you wanted to stop by and take a look at something after you're done here."

"Maybe. What is it?"

"I'm not sure. Something in the grain bin. A clue, maybe."

Beth smiled. "Of course. Can't you tell me more about it?"

"No, you have to see it. I understand if you're too busy."

"No, I'm not too busy. I only have one customer here, I think, so I'll stop by shortly."

Dave touched the rim of his cap and drove off.

Sunshine came strolling down the driveway, smiling, and waved.

"Hi, Beth," she said when she arrived. "I guess I should have called to tell you that you didn't have to come today. My parents are here, so I can use one of their cars to drive into Plato."

She seems pretty cheerful, Beth thought. *Maybe she doesn't know about Ruth and Lester.*

"Does that mean your phone has been turned on?"

"Yup, and the electricity. And my dad had a load of gravel spread on the driveway to fill in the potholes. They're spoiling me.

"I don't mind the extra stop. It's not far out of my way, and it's probably not worth changing the route if it's just for a short time. How long are your folks staying?" Beth said.

"For the rest of the summer," Sunshine said.

"As long as that? Then, maybe we will make a change."

"Yeah. Lester and I broke up, so my folks decided to stay and help me out with the baby. My dad is a teacher, so that works out for them."

Beth climbed into the bookmobile and Sunshine followed.

"Where's your little boy now?"

"He's in the house with my mom," Sunshine said.

"I see. I bet it's nice to have her around. And, I'm sorry about you and Lester," Beth said.

Sunshine frowned. "It's not the first time we broke up. He wanted me to take off with him and go to New York without money or a plan. From past experience, I knew we'd end up couch surfing or sleeping in a tent by the side of the road. I said no. I have my son to think about. So, he decided to run off with the neighbor lady."

"So, you know about him and Ruth?"

"Yeah, I know. He didn't hide it. He's always been kind of a tomcat. He says monogamy is passe."

Beth fiddled with the date-stamp, unsure of what to say. "Well, I'm sorry about that."

"You know what? I'm not," Sunshine said. "If he shows up again, maybe I'll tell him to keep moving. I think I can do better."

Sunshine started humming as she browsed through the books.

After she'd made her selection, Beth checked out her books, noted down her new phone number, and said she'd check on altering the bookmobile route for the summer.

"So, I'll probably see you in Plato next week," Beth said.

Then she headed back to the Cedar farm.

Chapter 32

August 11, 1969

Beth turned into the Cedar farm's driveway. Dave's truck was parked by the grain bin. As she parked the bookmobile, he came around the side of the truck and waved her over to join him outside of the grain bin access door. She hurried over.

"Hi, Dave. What did you want to show me?"

"I noticed an odd thing in there." He gestured toward the grain bin. "I can't quite figure out what it is. Do you want to take a look?"

"Okay." Beth smiled. It would be great to have a breakthrough to tell Logan and Evie about when they got together tonight.

He opened the access door and held out his hand. "After you." He helped her up onto the metal step below the door, and she climbed in. "Over there, on the other side." He pointed.

Beth climbed inside. It was stifling hot from the sun beating down on the metal exterior. It smelled of grain dust, with a trace of the bleach that Dave had used to clean up after Vern's body had been removed.

She started walking across the bin. "What am I looking for?" she called back over her shoulder.

The access door slammed shut. She turned, paused, then hurried back to the door and tried to push it open. It wouldn't budge. She waited for a moment, then banged on the door and called out. "Dave, the door blew shut. Can you open it?"

No response.

Her heart was beating faster, and she felt a bubble of panic rising in her chest. She put down her purse and hammered on the door with both fists and yelled, "Dave! Dave! Open the door!" The banging sound reverberated around her.

"I warned you, snoopy girl," he yelled back. "Now you can stay in there and die."

Beth heard him running away. Her mind whirled. So, he was the one who had sent her the note! She frantically looked around for another way out and spotted the ladder on the other side of the bin that led up to an access door in the roof.

There was a roar of machinery starting up, and grain started raining down on her from above. Apparently, Dave planned to bury her in grain.

Beth coughed as dust rose from the grain as it hit the floor. She removed the scarf she was wearing as a headband, tied it across her mouth, and ran to the ladder. The bottom rung was too high for her to get a foot on it. She grabbed onto the highest rung she could reach and ran her feet up the wall until she got both of her feet on the bottom rung. Then she started to climb, rung by rung, one at a time. Her hands were slippery with sweat, and her legs shook as she clung to the ladder. Her breathing was labored from the dust and the cloth covering her mouth. The wheat grains pelted her like hordes of stinging bees as they bounced off of the steel walls.

Once at the top, she tried to push open the roof hatch door. It wouldn't budge. She clung to the ladder with one hand while hitting upward with her other hand. It wouldn't open. It must be latched shut. Beth clung, panting, to the ladder. It was even hotter and dustier up here. It was just a matter of time until she was overcome by heat exhaustion and couldn't hang on any longer. Desperately, she searched for a way out.

At least there was a sliver of light around the edge of the hatch door. Maybe if she shouted, someone would hear her. After resting, she pulled the scarf down from her mouth and began to yell, "Help, help!" until she started coughing from the dust and pulled the scarf back up over her nose and mouth.

It was so loud in here that she could barely hear herself. How could anyone else hear her? She wondered. Outside, the auger, which was bringing grain up to the top of the bin, was banging and churning. Inside, the spinner on the roof was throwing the grain out sideways to distribute it evenly, and the grain was pinging and echoing as it bounced off the sides of the bin.

Beth didn't know how long she clung to the ladder, eyes closed, as the grain rattled past, just hoping and praying that she could hang on. Suddenly, she remembered the large screwdriver she'd stashed in her purse after using it to get into the storage facility in Grand Bend.

Her purse! She looked down. It was nowhere in sight. It must be buried where she'd dropped it inside of the access door. She hurried down the ladder to retrieve it. The grain was now about knee deep. She sprinted across the grain, her feet sinking with every step, as though being sucked down. It was like running through thick mud. She was panting by the time she reached the place where she'd dropped her purse. She fell to her knees and frantically started digging around as she sank into the grain. At last! Her fingers felt the strap. She grabbed hold of it and hauled it up.

Then, she struggled upright on the uneven surface while being pelted with grain. Once standing, she dug through her purse. There it was! It had sunk to the bottom. Gleefully, she remembered Evie's warning when she'd bought it in Dayton's, that if she had such a big bag, she would accumulate all kinds of things. She was right. But there was an advantage to hauling the heavy thing around, after all.

Beth dropped the screwdriver back in the bag, zipped it shut, slung it across her chest, and hurried back to the ladder. At least now she could more easily get a foot on the bottom rung. She quickly climbed back up to the top.

Drenched in sweat and panting, she rested there for a few moments. Then, she retrieved the screwdriver from her purse.

While clinging to the ladder with one hand, she jammed it into the airspace between the hatch and the roof and worked it around until she hit an obstacle. That must be the latch. She pushed on it. Nothing happened. Maybe she needed to try it from the other side.

She pulled out the screwdriver. But her hand was slippery with sweat, and she dropped it. She nearly burst into tears as she watched it land below. "Damnit! Damnit!" she yelled. Then, she paused and said out loud, "Calm down, Beth. You just have to go get it." She dried her hands on her shirt, one at a time, climbed down the ladder, retrieved it, and climbed back up.

She held onto the ladder with her left hand, her arm burning with fatigue, as she leaned out at an angle and wedged the screwdriver into the gap from the other side. She worked it around more quickly this time, since she knew where the latch was, until she felt the latch move. With a bit more pressure, she unlatched it. When she lifted the hatch door, a welcome burst of outside air greeted her. Beth pulled down the scarf covering her face and started to climb out when she heard a loud crack, and something whistled past her ear.

She looked below and saw Dave pointing a rifle at her. He was trying to kill her! She ducked back inside.

"Stay in there or I'll shoot you," he yelled up.

She clung to the top of the ladder, trying to calm her racing pulse and whirling mind and come up with a plan, but she couldn't focus. Her heart sank. She was trapped.

Then, she heard a new sound. Someone was climbing up the ladder on the outside of the building. He was coming to get her! Beth looked around wildly. There was no place to hide. If she climbed down, he would be able to get a good shot at her. Could she hide under the grain? No, he would see the lump in the grain, and she would probably suffocate if she tried that. She'd rather meet him on the top than let him shoot her like a fish in a barrel. With that thought, she climbed out of the hatch and onto the roof of the grain bin.

There was a railing around the hatch; she closed the hatch door and leaned against the railing. Her heart was beating wildly. In a few moments, Dave's head appeared at the top of the ladder. He had the rifle slung across his shoulder.

When he saw Beth, he grabbed it and pointed it at her heart. "Don't move. Or I'll shoot!" he said.

"Why are you doing this, Dave?" she asked, trying to sound calm.

"You know why. I killed that son-of-a-bitch, Vern. And good riddance too. But you just had to keep poking your nose into it. Didn't you?"

"You killed him, Dave? Why?"

"It was an accident. He was here on Saturday when I stopped by for a pack of smokes, and he started in on me about how the grain bin wasn't cleaned out to his liking. So, I got in there and started sweeping up. He climbed in after me and went on about how worthless I was and how he knew I had sent the threatening notes."

"You sent them?" Beth asked.

She noticed that Dave had lowered the rifle a bit. If she could keep him talking, maybe she could get it away from him.

"I just wanted to mess with his head. I saw him looking at the notes and muttering to himself. It was funny. It took him long enough to figure out it was me. I just took one of the pads he stole from the radio station." An evil grin formed on his face, showing off his yellow teeth. Then it faded. "Anyway, I knew he was up to something illegal, the way he was sneaking around. I followed him and saw him moving boxes of stuff around. I figured I should be paid for keeping my mouth shut."

"But he disagreed?" Beth asked.

"Said I could go to hell. Called me names, worthless scum, and the like. Said I was fired. I just lost it. I knocked him down, and he hit his head against the gearbox on the floor sweep."

"So, you tried to make it look like an accident," Beth said. "That's not murder. You won't be in big trouble for that But, if you shoot me, that's no accident. You'll be in prison for the rest of your life for that."

She could see the hesitation on his face as he lowered the rifle a bit more. Then, she heard the police sirens heading in their direction. Dave turned to look as two squad cars pulled into the driveway. As he did so, he moved his finger off of the trigger. Beth grabbed the barrel of the rifle, jerked it out of his hands, and threw it down to the ground.

Four police officers ran toward the grain bin, guns drawn, and ordered Dave to come down. As he slowly descended the ladder, Beth clung to the railing and waited. She tried to stand once, but her legs were too weak and shaky, so she sat back down.

After a while, she saw Dave loaded into a squad car.

Someone climbed up the ladder, and Bill's face appeared. "Beth, are you coming down?"

"Oh, hi, Bill. I don't know. It's kind of high up. Just give me a minute," she said.

"Do you want me to carry you?" he asked.

"You? Carry me?" Beth felt on the edge of hysteria and laughed too loudly and too long. When she calmed down, she said, "I'm not a kitten in a tree. I can manage."

She got up on still shaky legs and, while clinging to the railing, made her way to the ladder. Bill was waiting a few rungs down. He guided her foot to the first rung. Slowly they made their way down until they were standing on the ground.

"Okay now?" Bill asked.

"Yeah, I'm okay. Just really thirsty. You have no idea how hot it was in there. I need some water. Do you have any?"

"No, sorry."

"Never mind. I think I have some in the bookmobile." Beth looked at it wearily. "I suppose I should finish my route."

"Oh, I don't think you're in any state to do that. You can be excused, under the circumstances."

Beth looked at her dust and sweat-encrusted arms. "Yeah, I suppose you're right. But people will be waiting for me and will call the library. I should let Miss Tanner know what happened."

"Miss Tanner was the one who called us."

"She did?"

"Yeah. People were lighting up the phone lines on your behalf. Old Mr. Olson noticed something was wrong when your bookmobile didn't drive past his place the second time, and he heard some strange sounds coming from the Cedar farm. So, he called your dad. Your dad called the library, and Miss Tanner called us."

Bill walked Beth to the bookmobile. "Are you going to be okay to drive?"

"Sure. I'll just rest for a bit first."

Beth climbed up into the bookmobile. Bill followed her. She got a bottle of water out of the cooler.

"Want anything?" she asked.

"No thanks."

She sank down into the driver's seat, opened the bottle, and guzzled down the water in a few gulps. Nothing had ever tasted better!

"Okay then. I'll radio back that you're okay and that they should let the librarian know that you won't be completing your route today because you have to come down to the station to make a statement."

"How about if I go home first and clean up? I'm filthy."

"No problem. By the way, Logan is out on bail."

"Really? That is so great!" Beth sprang up and threw her arms up around Bill's neck and kissed him on the cheek. "Thanks, Bill. And, thanks for coming to my rescue."

He blushed up to the tips of his ears. "No problem. Just doing my job," he said, smiling down into her eyes.

Chapter 33

August 16, 1969

The first hints of autumn were in the air. The leaves of poplar, birch, and cottonwood trees were streaked with gold. A northwest wind brought with it a refreshing coolness and lower humidity and the scent of northern campfires. Parents rushed around town buying school supplies, and college students were filling out their schedules. Beth half-listened to the cicadas in the trees outside of the open windows, singing about the end of summer.

Beth, Evie, and Logan sat in their favorite booth at the Pig and Whistle, sipping beers, celebrating that all charges against Logan had been dropped.

"I can't believe that summer is almost over," Beth said. "We should get in at least one more trip to the lake while we can."

"We could go after we sign up for classes next week," Evie said. "I think that I'll just take one or two classes this quarter. I'm going to try to get a couple of back-to-back Tuesday and Thursday classes. I'll be busy in the theater, if ticket sales for our first show are any indication."

"That sounds like a good plan," Beth said.

I wish I could," Logan said. "But I can't get away. I lost three weeks while I was in jail. It's only four weeks until opening night, and we're minus a director and a cast member, since Ruth and Nigel dropped out."

"Did I tell you?" Beth said. "Miss Tanner wants to audition for Lady Bracknell. Apparently, she did some theater in college."

"Tell her to give me a call. If she fits the part, that would be great. I suppose I'll take over as director, but then I'll need to find someone to run the box office."

"That shouldn't be too hard," Evie said. "The community is really stepping up to support the theater."

"By the way, have I told both of you how grateful I am for everything you've done for me and keeping the theater going?" Logan asked.

"Only about a dozen times." Beth smiled. "I'm just glad it all worked out."

"I still have some questions," Evie said. "What about the eagle feather in your desk? Did you ever find out who put it there?"

Logan sighed. "Yeah, I did. It was Nigel. Man, I was so wrong about him. I thought he was a friend and that he was genuinely interested in helping start up a new theater. But he was just here for Ruth. When I caught him going through my desk drawers the other day, he confessed all, and then he quit."

"I wonder how he got involved in the whole smuggling operation," Evie said.

"I don't know for sure," Logan said. "But I bet it was Ruth's idea. She had both her husband and her boyfriend in on it. She probably wanted them to have more money to spend on her. She had expensive tastes."

"You might be right about that," Beth said. "Of course, she claimed she had no idea it was going on. But I don't see how that's possible."

"Nigel said that when Ruth dumped him, she told him that there was someone else. For some reason, he assumed it was me. To get even, he planned to implicate me and then drop out of the picture. But then things took another turn, as you know."

"They sure did," Beth said. "Was he the one who called the cops and said you were out there the day Vern was killed?"

Logan sighed again. "Yup. Fingering me for Vern's murder was an attempt to divert attention from himself. As Ruth's boyfriend, he would have been the natural suspect." Logan looked around to be sure no one was listening. "It didn't help that I went out that way to buy grass from Lester. Obviously, I couldn't tell that to the cops without getting myself, or Lester, in trouble. So, I said I was talking to Ruth. I did stop and talk to her, sometimes. But, on the day that Vern was killed, she was in the cities. So, my alibi didn't hold up. Lying to the cops really made me look guilty."

"And now she's run off with Lester." Evie laughed. "She must be at least ten years older than him."

"At least. I think she's pushing forty," Beth said. "It won't last. I bet she'll soon find someone she likes better."

"Poor Vern," Logan said. "There's something I never thought I'd say."

They all laughed.

"And poor Dave too," Beth said. "Although I didn't feel that way when he was pointing a rifle at me."

"I'll bet. You were lucky he didn't kill you," Logan said. "You should be more careful."

"I agree. That thought sort of occurred to me too." Beth laughed. "Well, enough about that. This is a celebration."

"Yeah," Logan said. "Let's order another round of drinks and crank up the jukebox."

They were prancing around to "Honky Tonk Woman" when Bill walked in. He cast an amused glance in their direction and headed to the bar.

"Hey, Bill," Logan called out, "come join the party."

"No thanks." He sat down at the bar and ordered a drink.

When the song ended, Logan and Evie started dancing to the next tune. Beth thought Bill look lonely, so she retrieved her drink and joined him at the bar.

"Is this seat taken?" Beth indicated the stool next to him.

"Nope."

The screen door slammed shut as a bunch of Logan's friends entered. They joined Logan and Evie. Everyone began talking at once, and the noise level in the bar went up.

"Why not join the party?" Beth asked.

"I don't think I'd be all that welcome," he said. "After all, I arrested him."

"He knows you were just doing your job."

"I suppose. But I'll give it awhile. How about you?"

"I'm not really a party animal. I'm a librarian in training, you know. I prefer a quiet and peaceful life."

Bill snorted. "Right! I guess that's why you ended up on top of a grain bin with a rifle pointed at you."

"Okay, so there are exceptions." Beth smiled. "Thanks again for rushing to my rescue. How did you manage to get there in the nick of time?"

"Fingerprints."

"What?"

"The threatening note you got. Remember? I ran the fingerprints, and they were Dave's."

"Dave's? So, he has a record?"

"Yeah. Just drunk driving. But, when I got word that you seemed to have gone missing between the hippie farm and the Olsons' place, I kind of put two and two together. Plus the fact that I'd told you to stay away from Ruth, and you're not good at following directions."

"I guess not." Beth sipped her beer. "I'll have to work on that. You know what you are?"

"What's that?"

"You're handy, sometimes."

Their eyes met in the mirror over the bar, and they smiled at each other.

Epilogue

September 12, 1969

It was opening night at the Majestic Theater, and the house was packed. Peeking through the curtain, Beth spotted Bill Crample, looking uncomfortable in a too-tight suit, sitting in the middle, a few rows back. Her family was seated on the aisle, near the back. Her sister-in-law, Debbie, was eight months pregnant, and they wanted to be able to make a quick exit if the baby decided to come early. There was a buzz of excitement as the lights went down, and the curtain rose.

In act one, Lady Bracknell, played by Miss Tanner, swept into Algernon's flat, fully decked out in late nineteenth century finery. Somehow, Jessie Hanson, the wardrobe lady, had managed to alter the costume to fit Miss Tanner, who was several inches taller and at least twenty pounds heavier than Ruth.

Miss Tanner hammed it up, eliciting laughs with almost every line. When she proclaimed that "To lose one parent, Mr. Worthing, may be regarded as a misfortune; to lose both looks like carelessness," the theater rocked with laughter.

Backstage, all went well until the high school volunteers, while moving the props between the first and second act, dropped the fireplace. The canvas and plywood construction fell apart. Beth and Evie rushed in to pick up the pieces. After a brief flurry of whispered conversations, the stage was set for the second act, in a garden in the country, with only a few minutes delay. Evie decided that they would just have to do without the fireplace for the drawing room scene in act three.

The rest of the play continued without incident and was a rousing success. The actors received a standing ovation for a job well done. The notoriety surrounding Vern's death and Logan's arrest hadn't hurt. If anything, it had helped ensure that virtually everyone in town knew about the new theater and its owner. Ticket sales for all performances were solid.

Logan threw a pizza party backstage after the show. All the cast and crew were invited, as well as a select group of supporters and potential donors. One of them was the lawyer, Mr. Nobis. He took a slice of pizza and some beer and joined Evie and Beth.

"Guess who got arrested?" he said.

"Who?" Beth and Evie said in unison.

"Lester Riggs."

"Lester Riggs? Who's that?" Beth asked.

"You know, Lester, of Lester and Ruth."

"Oh, right," Evie said. "Ruth's hippie boyfriend."

"Yes. But that didn't last," he said.

"I knew it wouldn't," Beth said. "Didn't I say so?"

"You did. You must have a crystal ball," Evie said. "So why didn't it last, and why did Lester get arrested?"

"Well, apparently, she dumped him and took off for New York City after the Woodstock concert."

"That I knew," Beth said. "Sunshine told me he called her to beg her to let him come home. She was trying to decide if she should."

"I guess she must have said it was okay," Mr. Nobis said. "Because he was on his way home with his tail between his legs when he got stopped for a speeding violation. The way I heard it, clouds of marijuana smoke billowed from the car when the cops stopped him. So, they searched the car and found a large bag of the stuff under a blanket in the backseat."

"Ah, poor Lester," Evie said.

They all laughed.

"Are you going to represent him?" Beth asked.

"No, it's not the kind of pro-bono case I'm interested in. But, in a way, it's a good thing for him," Mr. Nobis said.

"Why's that?" Beth asked.

"He's been dodging the draft. With a felony arrest, he won't have to worry about that anymore."

"It's funny how things work out. Isn't it?" Beth said.

Made in United States
Troutdale, OR
11/23/2024

25239452R00181